The man v... door wa... wea...

He tipped his black Stetson before handing her an envelope. "I've been asked to give you this."

Darcy tried to read the emotions in his dark brown eyes. Pity? Immediately she tore her gaze away and read the letter informing her of her parents' death.

"Are you all right?" Luke asked. His voice slid over her like a warm, soothing blanket, numbing the pain that threatened to spill out and destroy her thin veneer of calm.

"I'm sorry it took us so long to find you."

"That was the point," she murmured.

"Well, I did find you. And now I'm here to take you home to the ranch."

"The ranch." Darcy grimaced at the very thought of it. "I'm sorry, Mr. Lassiter. But there's nothing for me in Raven's Rest anymore." She met his startled gaze. "And I have no intention of ever going back."

Books by Lois Richer

Love Inspired

A Will and a Wedding #8
†*Faithfully Yours* #15
†*A Hopeful Heart* #23
†*Sweet Charity* #32
A Home, a Heart, a Husband #50
This Child of Mine #59

† Faith, Hope & Charity

LOIS RICHER

credits her love of writing to a childhood spent in a Sunday school where the King James version of the Bible was taught. The majesty and clarity of the language in the Old Testament stories allowed her to create pictures in her own mind while growing up in a tiny Canadian prairie village where everyone strove to make ends meet. During her school years, she continued to find great solace in those words and in the church family that supported her in local speech festivals, Christmas concerts and little theater productions. Later, in college, her ability with language stood her in good stead as she majored in linguistics, studied the work of William Shakespeare and participated in a small drama group.

Today, Lois lives in a tiny Canadian town with her husband, Barry, and two very vocal sons. And still her belief in a strong, vibrant God who cares more than we know dominates her life. "My writing," she says, "allows me to express just a few of the words God sends bubbling around in my brain. If I convey some of the wonder and amazement I feel when I think of God and His love, I've used my words to good effect."

This Child of Mine
Lois Richer

Published by Steeple Hill Books™

STEEPLE HILL BOOKS

Steeple
Hill™

ISBN 0-373-87059-0

THIS CHILD OF MINE

Copyright © 1999 by Lois Richer

Printed in U.S.A.

I am with you and will watch over you wherever you go, and I will bring you back to this land. I will not leave you until I have done what I have promised you.

—*Genesis* 28:15

To Darcy,
who constantly teaches me about
tenacity and following my own path.

Chapter One

~❧~

Darcy Simms stared in disbelief at the pink slip attached to her meager paycheck.

Laid off! How could she be laid off? She needed that job and the money it provided if she was going to survive. Where was the justice in laying her off now, of all times? How would she manage?

Darcy ignored the sound of the ringing telephone reverberating down the hall of the old, rundown apartment building. The thing was always ringing. But the calls were never for her. How could they be? She'd made very sure that her new life didn't involve anyone from her past, and her friends at work didn't know where or how she lived. They thought she was just like them—young and carefree.

What a joke!

The sudden pounding on her door sent her heart shifting into overdrive. That awful man down the hall had been watching her coming and going for the past week. His beady little eyes took in everything about her. She wondered if he was even now outside her door, waiting. Her gaze flew to the dead-bolt locks, to be sure they were fastened securely, even though she knew one good kick would easily splinter the tired old wood.

"Yes?" She called out finally when the banging resumed. She glanced just once toward the curtained bedroom. "What is it?"

"Darcy Simms?" The voice was low and hesitant, as if the owner weren't sure he had the right place.

"Y-yes." Darcy stood behind the door, waiting. Why would a man be outside her door? "What do you want?"

"I have something for you, Miss Simms. Would you please open the door?" The voice was firmer now, determined. The only good thing was that he didn't sound like her neighbor.

"Who are you? What do you want?" When there was no immediate answer, she panicked and backed away. "Go away or I'll call the police!" He couldn't know that she didn't have a telephone, could he?

"My name is Luke Lassiter, Miss Simms. Please. Just hear me out. I'm from Colorado. You might say your parents sent me."

"Then you're just a bit late." She laughed harshly. "And so are they. About five years too late, I'd say. Now go away."

"I can't. I promised that I'd do this and I intend to keep my word. I'll wait out here if you insist, but I *am* going to speak to you."

He waited a long time. As hard as she listened, Darcy could hear no impatient shuffling beyond the door. There was no sound of footsteps moving down the hall. It seemed that Mr. Luke Lassiter would not give up easily on this mission of his.

If that's who he really was. Images of yesterday's bloody fist fight in the corridor flew through her mind and Darcy cast another protective glance at the bedroom. But since everything was quiet for now, she decided to risk speaking to this man. Whomever he was.

"I'm going to undo the door just enough to talk to you—but the chain stays on."

"In this neighborhood, I don't blame you." The reply was agreeable. There was silence then and Darcy undid the top and bottom bolts loudly and noisily, pausing a moment before she finally opened the door.

Darcy peered through the crack in the door. Luke Lassiter was tall and lean and weathered looking. Dressed from head to foot in clean but worn denim, he wore a thick sheepskin-lined jacket to keep out the brisk November chill. Darcy doubted that the black Stetson on his head did much to keep his ears warm.

"Hello, ma'am," he drawled, tipping his hat. "I'm Luke Lassiter. I live just outside of Raven's Rest. I've been asked to give you this." He pulled a plain white envelope out of his pocket and handed it through the crack in the door. "It's from Reverend Anderson. He's the pastor out our way these days."

Something glowed out of his dark brown eyes. What was it? Pity? Darcy immediately tore her gaze away from his and slit the letter open.

"I can't imagine what your Reverend Anderson would have to—oh, no!" Darcy stared in horror at the words scrawled across the page in big black letters.

I regret to inform you that your parents, Martha and Lester Simms, were killed six weeks ago in a terrible car accident. We have spent some time searching for you in the hope that you might return home as your parents last requested. I trust this will be possible for you and urge you to have every confidence in my friend Luke Lassiter, who will be happy to accompany you on your return journey.

> Yours,
> Reverend David Anderson

Never—not once in the past five years since she'd shaken the dust of her hometown off her feet—had Darcy even considered not seeing her parents again. She'd wished a lot of things on those stern, unforgiving people. But not this. Never this!

"Would you please let me in now?" Darcy barely heard Luke's low-voiced request, and automatically moved to unsnap the chains that would allow him entry to her home. "Are you all right? Can I get you anything?" His voice slid over her like a warm, soothing blanket, numbing the pain that threatened to spill out and destroy her thin veneer of calm.

"No." She sank onto the ratty old sofa that sat on one leg and three coffee cans, and stared at the paper. "No, nothing. Thanks."

"I'm sorry that it took us so long to find you, Miss Simms." The tall cowboy folded himself until he was hunkered beside her. "There was no forwarding address, you see. Not much to go on."

"That was the point," she murmured dazedly, wondering now why it had mattered so much that she hide away in New York.

"I had no idea you were this far away until a friend of mine got a tip from the IRS about your tax records. I followed you home from the factory." He smiled grimly at her start of fear and surprise. "Well, we had to find you somehow." His smile was sympathetic. "There's the ranch and everything."

"Yeah, the ranch." She grimaced at the very thought of it. "Thank you for coming all this way and telling me, Mr. Lassiter. I appreciate the time and effort. But there's nothing for me in Raven's Rest anymore. And I have no intention of going back."

She fluttered the papers attached to Reverend Anderson's letter. "According to this they've been gone some time. I'm sure there's already been a funeral and my parents are buried in the local cemetery. There's nothing left for me to do."

"Not even to mourn?" His voice accused her of something, and Darcy couldn't help but let her hackles rise at the old pattern from the past repeating itself. *Ungrateful daughter.*

"I did mourn, Mr. Lassiter. Five years ago, when I left good old Raven's Rest and its narrow-minded citizens. On that day I vowed I'd never return. I see no reason to go back and dig up the past. I have to move on."

"What about the ranch?"

"What about it? It's not my home. It never was. It was merely a place I stayed until I could get away."

She stood and marched over to the sink, intent on drying the three plastic dishes she'd used for supper, if only to get away from the knowing look in Mr. Lassiter's piercing dark eyes.

"So what's stopping you from coming back—just one last time? To hear the will and dispose of what's left." She figured that he'd noticed the jerk of her shoulders at the word "will" and pressed on that one weak spot. "It's their final word on the only earthly goods they had to leave you, Darcy. It's your heritage—"

"Mommy, mommy!"

Darcy whirled, eyes wide with surprise as four-and-a-half-year-old Jamie raced across the room and grabbed her around the knees.

"I had a bad dream," he cried, staring at Luke Lassiter with that immediate intensity that all children possess. "There was a bad man." His eyes were huge pools of violet as he stared at their guest.

"Hi, little guy," Luke said, bending down slightly to meet the boy's gaze. "I'm not a bad man. I'm one of the good guys. Come to take you and your mommy for a ride to a ranch that's far, far away. Would you like that?"

To Darcy's surprise, her shy, introverted son left her embrace to walk over and stand in front of their guest.

"Yes, I would," he said clearly, arms folded across his chest. "Are there horses?"

"A ranch always has horses." Luke watched as the little boy stared wide-eyed at his scuffed cowboy boots. "Maybe I could even take you for a ride. If it's okay with your mom.'' He twisted his head to study her. "Is it okay, Mom?''

"I don't know. I'll have to see.'' She gave him her most furious look, hoping he understood how difficult he was making it for her. "You have no right,'' she whispered angrily as Jamie moved away.

"*He* does,'' Luke asserted gravely. "He has a right to see the heritage that you're so intent on giving up.''

"I'm not giving it up. It was never mine.'' She let the bitter smile curve her lips. "Perhaps you didn't get the whole picture, Mr. Lassiter. My parents didn't know what to do with me. I wasn't exactly what they expected.''

"How do you know that?'' He sank down into the rickety armchair with an ease that Darcy envied.

"Believe me, I learned early on that a scruffy tomboy was the last thing Martha and Lester expected. They should have gotten a boy, or at least a dainty, little girl who would have accepted all their rules and settled down with a nice local boy.''

"And that wasn't you?'' He looked genuinely interested, Darcy decided. That in itself was unusual. Her life was something less than interesting.

"Hardly.'' She grimaced. "I'm five feet nine inches, Mr. Lassiter, and no one has ever called me dainty. Besides, I never could learn to sit still for hours on end while some man stood in the pulpit, berating people for being human.''

"Are you sure that's what he was doing?''

Darcy stared at him. "Maybe you had to be there.'' She shrugged. "It was doom and gloom. All the time. Feel guilty, you sinner. Ask forgiveness. Repent. Evil, wrong, no good. That's all I ever heard.''

"Sounds pretty bad," Luke Lassiter agreed, smiling. "Can't say it's my idea of a good service either."

Darcy stared. "You think it's funny? Believe me, there was no joy there."

"No, I don't imagine there was," he murmured gently. "But then a lot of people feel that way about God. They haven't found the real meaning of love, I guess."

"And what, pray tell, is the *real* meaning of love?"

"I don't think it's something you can explain. It's something you have to feel as it heals you."

"Love doesn't heal. It just hurts people, makes them obligated to someone else when they should be free to live their own lives." Darcy couldn't disguise the acid edge to her voice.

"Yeah, sometimes love hurts. Nobody said life was without pain. But it can also heal and renew and rejuvenate. Love isn't ever wasted."

The very idea was a whole new concept in Darcy's young life, especially since she'd wasted twenty-three long years loving people who couldn't possibly love her back.

"Can you be ready to leave tomorrow morning? I don't like to be away too long," he asked, interrupting her thoughts.

"From the farm?" Darcy remembered well that a rancher's dedication to his cattle was par for the course in Raven's Rest. Sometimes, she remembered bitterly, it even exceeded a father's duty to his own family.

"Well, there's that." Luke grinned at Jamie as he piled up blocks on the floor and then swatted them down. "But actually, I was thinking of my Aunt Clarice. She's all alone and I worry about her."

"Clarice?" Darcy frowned. "I don't remember any Clarice at Raven's Rest."

"Ah, but you've been gone five years, haven't you," he reminded her with a smile. "Things change. Even at Raven's Rest."

"Nothing about that one-horse, narrow-minded, little town could change enough to make me want to live there again." Darcy laughed angrily. "I'm sorry, Mr. Lassiter, but I have no intention of going back."

"Why?" He glanced around the room, assessing its ugliness. His inquisitive eyes fell on the pink slip she'd laid on the table before answering the door. "There's nothing here holding you back, is there?" His gaze was steady, daring her to deny what he'd already surmised.

"Don't worry, I'll get another job," she told him defiantly. "I've managed this long."

"But there's no need. Why not take a break? Just for a while. You could relax on the ranch until the will has been sorted out. New York's not going anywhere."

His tone was smooth and cajoling and Darcy ached to give in. She was tired, desperately tired of just barely managing. It would be nice to release that tight control over things, even if only for a little while. Nice not to have to be on guard every moment of the day. She glanced at her son and smiled, thinking of the freedom of running in a yard of grass instead of the asphalt playground he was confined to at the day care.

And then the memories resurfaced from a time

she'd tried so hard to forget. In five years that awful feeling of loss hadn't lessened one whit. "I can't," she muttered finally. "I just can't."

"Sure you can." He was so sure of himself, his eyes calm but serious. "You just take it one day at a time and trust that somehow God will work it all out."

"Like He's done so far, you mean?" Her eyes mocked the ugliness of the dingy room and its thread-bare furnishings. "You'll understand if I find that a little difficult to do."

Luke Lassiter covered her hand with his. "I didn't say it would be easy." He smiled. "I just said you could do it."

Darcy didn't understand any of this. She didn't want to. What good would be served by rehashing the agony of the past?

She glared at him, gathering Jamie in her arms. "Why are you so interested? I don't mean anything to you."

"Of course you do. You're the daughter of some friends of mine and you're alone. Right now I think you could use a break." A funny look drifted across Mr. Lassiter's eyes as Jamie leaned his head against her legs and yawned noisily.

"I think Jamie needs some special time with his mom and maybe a place where he can run and yell to his heart's content. Raven's Rest certainly has enough room."

He hadn't said a word about the pathetic little apartment or the perpetual odor of boiled cabbage that seemed to hang in the air, but Darcy knew Luke Lassiter hadn't missed a single detail of the ugliness of her life.

"I have to put him back to bed." She said the words softly, as Jamie's eyes began to close. "Have a seat if you want." She padded across the floor and slipped behind the curtain to lay Jamie in the cot next to hers. He smiled in his sleep, shifting a little under the coarse woolen blanket.

"At least I did one thing right," she muttered to herself as tears of tiredness welled in her eyes.

"He's a wonderful little boy." The voice came from behind her left shoulder. "They look so innocent when they're sleeping, don't they?"

"Do you have children?" she asked, frowning.

"I did." The words were so soft that she barely caught them. The look on his face spoke of immense sadness, and Darcy couldn't deal with that. Not now.

"You didn't have to follow me in here," she whispered. "I'm not going anywhere. Not tonight at least." Urging him out of the room, she pulled the curtain into place. "And I don't think I'll be going anywhere tomorrow. Raven's Rest just isn't the place for me anymore."

"It doesn't have to be permanent. It's just while the will is settled and the estate disposed of. People will understand why you're there and that you need some time and space." His voice dropped. "Can't you do even that for your parents?"

"Why should I?" Darcy glared at him bitterly. "What difference could it possibly make now?"

Luke Lassiter's face was all shadows and inscrutability. But she could see the understanding in his eyes as he met her glance squarely. "Why not? What would it hurt you? They're dead now, Darcy. Your parents are gone. They can't hurt you anymore."

"They don't have to. They did a pretty good job while they were alive."

"But they're dead now."

The starkness of those words drilled a hole straight through to her heart. She'd wanted to come back to her hometown triumphant, successful. She'd wanted to show her parents that she had survived—prospered even—without them. And now, suddenly, everything she'd done, striven for for so long, was futile. She was never going to hear the words she'd waited for. What did it matter whether she kept her pride and stayed holed up in this dump or relaxed on the old homestead for a few days. No one could force her to do anything anymore. She'd left all that behind five years ago.

"Come back, Darcy. Rest for a while. Stay with Aunt Clarice and me. Let her coddle you and that little boy for a bit. Get a new start, a new perspective on things. I guarantee you won't be sorry."

His eyes held hers steadily as his voice cajoled her. His hand on her arm added strength to his words, and all at once Darcy knew she had to give in. To just let go and forget about pretending to be strong. It would be so wonderful to lean on someone else. Maybe she really was going to get a second chance.

God's got something in mind for you, Darcy. Was it only yesterday that her friend Mona had told her that? "I don't know what it is. I just know that He wants you to let Him be your father." Could dear, sweet Mona have known something about the future?

Was this some sort of heavenly sign? The timing of the layoff was rather convenient, wasn't it?

Darcy snorted at her own silliness. This wasn't any spiritual mission. This was just a simple matter of cleaning up loose ends. Tending to business while she dealt the old hometown a few facts. Nothing more.

"All right." Darcy tamped down the doubts and agreed at last. "I'll go." She sighed heavily. "I'm sure not promising to stick around for more than a couple of days. But I'll go back long enough to hear the will and give the old place one last glance. Satisfied?"

"More than satisfied." He grinned boyishly, and the smile wiped years off his face, making him seem like one of her cohorts from the old days. "I'll be by in the morning to pick you up. What time will you be ready?"

Darcy stared at him in surprise. "In the morning? But I have to give notice on this place and all sorts of things!" She saw his eyes narrow and knew what he was thinking. "I'm not backing down. I just need a little time." She handed him his Stetson.

"All right." He scratched his chin thoughtfully. "But I can't wait long. I'll pay whatever notice needs to be covered." He held up a hand at her protest. "The tickets aren't open-ended so I'll have to call the airline and see what's available after lunch. Will you have a lot of luggage?"

"There's nothing much worth taking, as you can very well see." She stood stiffly by the door. "But I don't intend to leave behind a mess for someone else to clean up. I'll throw out what I don't take. Most of it's junk anyway. After lunch will be fine.'' She opened the door and stood waiting.

"Great! I'll see you at one.'' He was almost through when he stopped in front of her. "I forgot. My aunt sent a few things with me. I left them in my hotel room. I'll bring them along.''

"Things?'' She frowned, wondering what kind of woman this Aunt Clarice would turn out to be. "I don't even know her.''

His laughter was a deep burst of pleasure that resounded down the long, dark hallway. "That wouldn't stop her.'' He chuckled. "If Aunt Clarice feels the Lord tells her to do something, she does it. No questions asked.''

Inwardly, Darcy groaned. A busybody, she decided. And probably a bossy one. Just what she needed to make her return to Raven's Rest complete.

"Actually, I think there are some dresses and stuff. She wasn't too specific.'' He stood looking down at her for a long time. Darcy shifted uncomfortably, hating being scrutinized so closely. She lifted a nervous hand to the tangle of curls that covered her head. "See you tomorrow,'' he said at last.

"Good night.'' Darcy closed the door behind him and bolted it carefully. She waited, listening for the tapping sounds of his booted heels as he walked away.

I've done it now, she told herself later as she lay in her sagging narrow bed. She stared up at the water-stained ceiling, fear and trepidation battling for supremacy in her mind.

Trust God, Luke had said. Darcy wanted to laugh

but the fear inside went too deep. She'd long since given up depending on God to help her, but Luke wasn't to understand about all that. No, she was on her own and she would manage. Somehow.

Still, it would be a break. She wouldn't have to look for a new job right away or stretch her money for day care. Best of all, Jamie could have some time away from the grit and grime of the city in winter. She wanted that more than anything. Maybe they would even celebrate Christmas this year.

Not that I'm taking anything back, she whispered, eyes squeezed closed. *I still think You abandoned me when I needed You the most. And I'm not going to forget that.*

The noises of the night closed around her as car horns honked and someone upstairs stamped on the floor. Scuffling footsteps and grunts of pain sounded from outside her door.

At least I've been lucky so far, she told herself. It's probably a good time to get out.

She giggled nervously at the silly thought, her fingers closing around the prickly, abrasive fabric of her surplus-store blanket.

Lucky? Who was she kidding? She was the unluckiest person alive. And going back to Raven's Rest was an undertaking only a fool would attempt.

Chapter Two

With a tentative hand, Luke flipped through the rack of dresses, disgusted by the skimpy fabrics and suggestive necklines. Aunt Clarice would have his hide if he got anything like this for Martha's daughter. He walked out of the department store and headed for a women's store across the way. But he had to get something. He'd promised Clarice that he would buy a few things.

"Just in case she feels like she doesn't want to come back here looking poorer than when she left." Clarice had insisted, stuffing a wad of money into his palm. "I have a feeling she needs help, Lucas. Lord knows, she can't have had an easy time of it. You get her a few really nice things."

"Aunt Clarice, I don't know anything about women's clothes! I won't have a clue what to buy."

"You'll do fine, son. I'll ask the Lord for a little heavenly guidance." Aunt Clarice was a great believer in the Lord imparting heavenly guidance to his children. Luke just hoped heaven had heard her orders.

"Sir? May I help you?" a friendly-looking saleswoman asked.

"My aunt sent me to buy some things for a friend." He explained what he wanted—some nice but sturdy clothes that would withstand life on a ranch. "And maybe some things she could wear to church or a social," he added at the last minute.

The saleswoman nodded and began her search. "What size is your friend?"

"Size?" Luke frowned. "I don't know. She's tall and slim."

"Hmm. That's not much to go on. Come with me for a moment." He followed the woman to the front of the store and stood behind her as she gazed out at the passing crowds. "That woman in the short skirt. Is she about that size?"

"Nope, smaller." Luke searched again. "There, that one with the dog. See her? Blond hair all piled up. Darcy's that size, I think." He studied the woman again. "Yeah, she looks about right. Darcy's got shorter dark hair though. And blue eyes. Sad blue eyes." He stopped then, suddenly aware of the curious look the woman gave him.

"A size seven, I'd say." The woman nodded. She began pulling out warm fuzzy shirts, denim skirts and thick bright sweaters. "These are the latest fall colors, and with that dark hair, she'll look beautiful in them." Soon a vast array of outfits lay spread out across the counter.

"If you mix and match them, you can get quite a bit of mileage out of these things," the woman assured him, holding up a pure white angora sweater and matching skirt. "And we've got a sale on. Of course, jeans would go with any of these."

"Fine, I'll take them all." Luke watched as she folded each garment. "Be sure the tags are off, will you? And maybe you could give me a box instead of those bags. I don't want her to know I just bought them."

"Of course." The woman looked as if this was a perfectly normal request. "Just let me check." She disappeared for a moment and then returned. "I'm sorry, I haven't a box the right size. But Gina's across the way stocks suitcases. Maybe that would be more appropriate. That way, it would look like you brought them with you from—where? Texas?"

Luke grinned. "Colorado. I'll be right back." He started down the aisle, but stopped when the woman called out.

"I know it's presumptuous," she told him, winking. "But I'm going to suggest it anyway. Gina has a lovely leather handbag that would tie in so perfectly with the leather bits on this vest and skirt. You might want to have a look at it."

And so it happened that Luke arrived at Darcy's with his own small overnight bag and a much larger one that he presented to her. "This is from Aunt Clarice. The plane doesn't leave until four so if you want to repack things, we have time. Hi, chum!" He lifted the grinning little boy into his arms and swung him up high. "Are you ready to go for a ride?"

"Yes, a plane ride. Mommy tol' me. We go up in the clouds." He pushed to get down, and Luke set him on the floor. "Mommy? Mommy, you're cry-ing."

"No, sweetie. I just got a bit of dust in my eye." She dashed away the tears and looked up at Luke. "I can't possibly take these," she told him. "They're worth a fortune."

"Well, I'm not wearing 'em!" He frowned down at her, frustrated that he'd picked out clothes she ob-viously hated. "You'd better take it up with Aunt Clarice. Although—" he pretended to study the array of bright colors "—I don't think there's much here that's her style. She mostly wears jeans." He picked up the royal blue anorak he'd chosen especially to go with her eyes. He fingered its cozy fleece lining be-fore holding it out.

"I'd put this on, though. It'll be mighty cold when we get off that plane. I'm sorry if they're not what you'd wear. Aunt Clarice probably has different ideas about women's clothes than you do."

"Are you kidding? They're wonderful!"

Luke watched as she slid one small hand over the silky soft material. He could see the look of longing before her eyes moved to the dowdy brown tweed hanging behind the door.

"I'll pay her back," she whispered, slipping her arms into the sleeves as he held it out. "However long it takes."

"Please, don't." He noted the spark of life in her tired eyes and how those pale cheeks seemed to glow now. "Clarice would be hurt. If you don't want all of them, that's all right. Maybe we can return them or something." He fingered the envelope with the tags stuffed inside his coat pocket.

"But she'd be really hurt if you tried to pay her for them. I know—why don't you just do something nice for her sometime." He didn't miss the way her fingers lingered on the soft cashmere. Luke had already noticed that Jamie's clothes were far newer than her own and in very good repair.

"But why would she do this? I don't mean anything to her. We don't even know each other." Darcy stared at him, face perplexed. "What does she want from me?" She pulled out the knitted gloves that he'd stuffed in the pocket.

Luke could see the puzzlement in her eyes and prayed for guidance as he tried to explain. "Aunt Clarice doesn't want anything *from* you, Darcy. She's trying to make you feel welcome. It's just the kind of thing she does." That wasn't very clear. He tried again.

"Clarice thinks God means for her to touch as many people's lives as she can, and so she tries to do that the best way she can. I guess this time she decided buying you those clothes would be right. She'd tell you He told her to do it."

There was a long drawn-out silence, and Luke waited for her decision, hoping God would forgive him for phrasing it in just that way.

"All right. I'll accept them. For now." Darcy looked dubious but she quickly tore open the paper bags at her feet and with several swift movements had tucked the contents inside. They were mostly Jamie's clothes, Luke noticed, with only a couple of shirts and a pair of jeans for herself.

"I don't have many clothes," she told him defensively. "We always wore uniforms."

"Really cuts down on what you need, doesn't it?" Since when did factory workers wear uniforms, he wondered? Luke motioned down toward his own case. "I figured that out when I left the navy. One little duffel bag was all I had." He pulled a package out of his pocket. "This truck is for Jamie. Should I wait until we're on the plane?"

She nodded. "Maybe you should keep it till then. He could play with it while we travel. He's already pretty excited." She cast one more glance around the ugly room and then picked up her purse. "I'm ready to go."

"The furniture?"

"Comes with the place. Such as it is. Do you want to call a cab?"

"There's one waiting." He watched silently as she gathered her son's hand firmly into her own. "If you open the doors, I'll manage the bags."

A big burly man stopped them at the bottom of the stairs. "Leaving, Sleeping Beauty?" he muttered, his words slurred.

"Yes, I'm moving. Here's the key, Mr. Munson. You can keep my damage deposit in lieu of notice." She met his gaze head-on, but Luke saw the ripple of fear that shook her and the panic that flew into her blue eyes.

"That's too bad, honey. You ain't seen much of anything but that room of yours." The man reached out as if to touch Jamie's hair, and the little boy pushed behind Luke, who quickly stepped forward and set down the cases.

"I think she's seen more than enough." He said it

quietly but clearly enough to ensure his meaning. "Please move back. We have a cab waiting."

The beady black eyes seemed to assess Luke's height and lean physique. "Yeah, sure," he muttered, stepping backward.

"Thanks." Luke ushered the woman and child through the door and down the steps to the waiting car. While the cabbie hoisted their bags into the trunk, Luke helped Darcy in and set Jamie in beside her. As the car drove away, he could clearly hear her sigh. Of relief? "Has he bothered you before?"

"No," she said softly. "But I don't think it would have been much longer. This isn't a place for single women." Her fingers unclenched from around the handles of her bag and she glanced up at him with the beginning of a smile at the corner of her wide, expressive lips. "Thanks."

Luke tipped his hat. "My pleasure," he grinned, only looking away after she did. The city flashed by him in a kaleidoscope of sights and sounds. Jamie scrambled onto his knees to get a better look as they rode for a while in silence.

"Mommy, I'm hungry." The little boy tapped his stomach. "My food box is empty."

Luke burst out laughing. "So's mine, kiddo. Bone dry." He guessed from the fleeting look in Darcy's eyes that she wasn't averse to eating either. "How about if we have a little snack when we get to the airport?"

"But won't they serve food on the plane?" She frowned, her eyes clouded. Probably figuring the cost, Luke decided.

"Airline food?" He shook his head, making a face.

"Not for *this* boy. I need good wholesome nourishing grub that sticks with you. Not six packets of peanuts and a few pretzels with some fancy water in a bottle!"

Darcy laughed at his indignant look, the sound tinkling in the car interior. "Pardon me! And airport food is any better?"

"We're not eating just any airport food," he told her, winking. "We're going to sample the finest of the fine—as children's menus go." Luke felt suddenly young again as he cajoled these two solemn souls into a bit of fun. "What do you like to eat, Jamie?"

"Noodle soup!" Jamie grinned happily. "With lots of crackers. And chocolate milk."

"Done. And you, madame?" He glanced across at Darcy, only to find his face enclosed by a pair of tiny cold hands. He turned back to Jamie. "What is it, son?"

"I don't know what to call you." The simple little request reminded Luke of another child who'd sat on his lap just three years ago. Younger than this, but filled with as many questions.

"Luke," he said around the lump in his throat. "Or Lucas. That's what Aunt Clarice calls me."

"Mister Luke is a nice name. Isn't it, Mommy?" The little boy beamed happily, peering up at his mother for confirmation.

"Very nice," she murmured, her eyes meeting Luke's. "And I like soup, too."

Because it's cheap, Luke guessed, but didn't say the words. Instead he teased her. "Oh, no. Soup is for the kids only. The adults have to have something awful like roast beef and mashed potatoes or deep-fried chicken. I'll give you some time to choose.''

She waited until Jamie was busy playing with a button on his coat before asking the question that lurked in the back of her eyes. ''Why are you being so nice to us? We don't mean anything to you.''

''Sure you do.'' He countered her quietly. ''You're Martha and Lester's daughter. And I owe them a huge debt of gratitude.''

''Why?'' She frowned as if she couldn't believe that her parents could have done anything good.

''Because once, not that long ago, they dragged me out of my stupor and back into reality. If it hadn't been for your parents and Aunt Clarice treating me like a son, I don't know where I'd have been. I want to do something to feel like I've at least paid a little of the debt I owe them.''

''You don't owe me anything, Luke,'' she whispered, her eyes once more reflecting that stark pain he'd glimpsed earlier. ''And especially because of them. If they could make you a part of the cold little world they inhabited, then I'm glad. Because they never did it for me.''

Luke studied the slim, hunched form with the haunted eyes, as a thousand thoughts raged through his brain.

Help me, Lord, he said silently. *There's so much hurt there. Shine Your healing love into her life.*

The cabbie pulled up just in time to prevent further discussion. Darcy clung to Jamie's hand as Luke carried the bags into the airport terminal, motioning her toward the nearest desk. Once they'd checked the luggage and received their boarding passes, they were free for over an hour.

"We don't have to be at the gate for a while. Let's find someplace to eat." Jamie begged to eat at the first fast-food place they came to, and Luke readily agreed, wanting to give the boy a treat. He could well imagine that little Jamie had not eaten out often.

"What are they called again, Mister Luke?" Jamie asked the same question for the fifth time, his fat little hand clutching the chicken tightly.

"Nuggets. Chicken nuggets. Do you like them?"

"Yes! Better than soup. I like these, too." The boy popped several fries into his grinning mouth and munched happily.

"And how about you, Darcy? Are you enjoying your meal?" He watched as the startled blue eyes lifted from her silent contemplation of the towering triple-burger on the plate in front of her.

"It's, uh, very nice," she murmured. "But how do you ever get a bite out of that without getting it all over?"

"That's half the fun." He chuckled, lifting up his own. "And that's one advantage of eating at a mostly kids' place. Nobody notices the mess!" He wiped the sauce off his chin as if to emphasize his point.

Darcy, shrugged, slipped out of her new blue coat and set it carefully behind her. Tucking a napkin onto her lap, she carefully lifted the concoction with both hands and took a dainty nip from the edge.

"Not like that!" Luke laughed as she dabbed at her lips. "You've got to get your mouth around it or all the good stuff will fall out the other side." He took a gigantic bite just to show her.

Darcy shook her head. "Too messy," she said, and proceeded to separate the layers and make two burgers out of the one. Then she lifted a piece to her mouth, grinning up at him as she bit into it. "Now *this* is a burger," she told him smugly.

Luke crunched away on the extra dill pickles he'd ordered, content to watch her face light up. "Do you want some of these?" He offered the plate. "Pickles are my favorite food. They form their own separate food group, you know."

"I've heard an argument very similar to that from Jamie," she giggled, taking one. "Only it had to do with chocolate bars." She raised her eyebrows. "He didn't win."

"Ah, well. But now he's got me on his side. We're a formidable force." Luke smiled, sipping his coffee.

"Isn't this the greatest coffee?" She blew across the mug and then delicately sipped the steaming brew. "I love freshly brewed coffee with a dollop of real cream."

"That isn't real cream. That's some junk they imported and reconstituted. On the ranch we have real cream. But I like it on pumpkin pie the best." He leaned back, enjoying the sight of two hungry people cleaning their plates. "The beef's fresher, too," he told her.

"In fact, everything's better in Colorado, right?" She laughed out loud at his frown of dismay. "I've heard it before. My dad thought that anybody who lived outside of the state had truly missed out on the best part of life." She said it automatically, without thinking. It was only after the words were spoken that she realized what she'd said. "He never wanted to see or hear about anything else," she whispered, her face pale.

"Well, it is a good thing to be content with your lot in life." Luke murmured it diplomatically, glancing down at Jamie, who was studying his mother's sad face. "But I think it's a good thing to broaden your horizons, too."

Darcy pushed away the remains of her burger, and leaned back in her chair. He could see the defiance in the tilt of her head and winced at the flash of those intensely blue eyes.

"Did you get along with my father?"

It wasn't what he'd expected, but Luke answered her. "Yes, pretty much. He was getting tired of doing it all himself, and by the time I came along, Lester had some problems that made the heavy work almost impossible for him."

She frowned. "I didn't know. But then why would I?" She shrugged almost carelessly, but Luke knew it was to hide the pain that he could see in her eyes.

"Lester talked about you all the time," he told her, hoping this was the right tack to take.

"He did? Why would he talk about me?"

"Well, it started when I asked him to sell a couple of the horses he had. He didn't ride anymore, and I figured it was costing too much money to keep feeding them all winter long." Luke tilted back on his chair, staring across the crowded restaurant. "He wouldn't hear of it. They were *your* horses, he said. Left in his care. When you came back, he wanted to be sure they were there, waiting for you. He spent hours currying them."

Luke saw the quick rise of tears in her clear blue

eyes and the downward tilt of her head as she tried to hide the evidence.

"I didn't know."

"Of course you didn't. It was his dream, anyway. Not yours." Luke wiped Jamie's hands and face and gave him a dollar to buy an ice cream at the nearby counter. "He'll be fine," he murmured when Darcy shifted, ready to follow. "We can see from here." They watched as the boy proudly presented his money and waited for the treat. "Your mother would have adored him."

"He looks a bit like her," Darcy said, then pursed her lips. "There's no point," she told him fiercely as she straightened her shoulders. "So you can just stop it. I'm not going to forget the past that easily, no matter how wonderful you make it sound. It was never a rose garden."

"Life seldom is," he agreed quietly. *Somehow, someway, Lord,* he prayed. *Break through that shell of pain and let her see the love of Your light. Let her know that You are there. Waiting.*

Chapter Three

Nothing had changed, Darcy reflected as she peered through the windshield of the half ton and watched the familiar landmarks pass by. Lookout Point, Pike's Pond, Willow Woods—it all sat there, waiting to bring back memories she'd stifled for so long.

"The house looks different," she said to Luke once they reached the old two-story. "It seems bigger."

"It is. Lester and I built a sunroom on the west side and he put a hot tub in the new master bedroom on the main floor."

"A hot tub?" Darcy frowned. Her father had hated excess. He'd scrimped and saved for as long as she could remember. Sometimes he'd overdone it and they'd gone without when they could have afforded some small luxuries. "Why a hot tub?"

"Your mother's arthritis got very bad." Although he said the words quietly enough, Darcy shifted uneasily. Was he blaming her? "Her hands particularly, although her knees and feet pained her a lot. When your dad saw how much the hot water at the nursing home helped her, he decided to get one out here so she wouldn't have to go into town for the treatments. She loved it.''

"She used to say that she could tell the weather by the joints in her fingers," Darcy told him. She roused herself from the saddening thoughts. "It looks like there's something new on the other end, too."

"Yes. We added a couple more bedrooms. When Clarice and I came, we were prepared to stay somewhere else, but your parents wanted us on the premises." He stopped abruptly. "I hope you don't mind. We've kept to the same arrangements. There's Aunt Clarice."

Darcy stared at him, wondering at the odd tone in his voice. "Of course not. I imagine you need to be close to keep things running. I'm sure that's what my parents would have wanted."

She peered through the gloom at a thin, tall woman who stood in the doorway, illuminated from behind by a blaze of house lights. When Luke pulled up in front of the building, she caught a glimpse of gray hair combed back from a face with piercing eyes, high cheekbones, a long straight nose and thin lips. Strangely enough, it was the warmth of her smile that held Darcy's attention.

"I'm Clarice Campion." Luke's aunt introduced herself as Darcy got out of the car. "It's an old French name—means mushroom or something like that. Come in, come in, my dear. Oh, a little boy!" Clarice peered down into Jamie's sleepy face. "What a handsome fellow. The spitting image of Martha. You carry him, Luke," she ordered brusquely, sliding her fingers under Darcy's arm. "He's too heavy for her. Come on, girl."

"Yes, ma'am." Luke grinned at them both and scooped the little boy up. "Okay, champ. We're home."

The air was frosty, and Darcy was glad to hurry up the steps and scoot inside. Until she looked around. It was the same. Exactly the same. Yes, a room or two had been added, but basically this was the same cold, hateful house she'd grown up in. She shrugged away the memories and closed the door behind Luke while reminding herself that the past was the past. This was supposed to be a new beginning.

"Lit a fire an hour ago," Clarice informed them, lifting the jacket from Darcy's shoulder. "Lovely color, this. On you," she added at the last moment.

"All due to you and I need to say thank-you," Darcy murmured, staring up into the hawk-like features. "The clothes you sent are lovely and I really appreciate them. But you spent far too much."

"Nonsense! What in the world is money for if not to spend?" Clarice nodded her head sternly. "No good socking it away in some moldy old bank. Doesn't do a body a bit of good there. Why not use it to give some joy? Hope you like them." The words came out clipped and sharp, but there was a twinkle in the black button eyes that warmed Darcy's heart just a bit.

"Did you ever tell my father your views?" Darcy wondered aloud, grinning at the heresy of waste that Lester Simms had preached against all during her childhood.

"Certainly! Told him many times. Came to see I

was right, too. Just had to break through that shell of
his. Wonderful giving man underneath. Sorry about
your loss.'' Clarice patted Darcy's hand firmly. ''No
point in fussing, though. They're in heaven and the
good Lord is treating them just fine.'' Clarice motioned her into the living room. ''Warmer here. Sit
down. Tea coming.'' Seconds later she whisked from
the room and into the kitchen.

''Mommy?'' Jamie, finally awake, pressed himself
down from Luke's arms and looked around worriedly.
''Is this Mister Luke's ranch?''

''This is where we're going to stay for a little
while, honey,'' she told him softly, removing his
jacket and brushing down his wayward strands of
hair. ''I used to live here when I was a little girl.''

''I hope it doesn't bring back too many unpleasant
memories.'' Luke watched as she hugged the little
boy close. ''Coming home, I mean.''

''The past can't hurt me anymore,'' she told him
bitterly. ''I've put it all behind me. I had to. Anyway,
it *is* the past.''

Clarice came in then, bearing a loaded tray with
sandwiches, a dish of pickles and beverages, so Darcy
didn't hear exactly what he muttered. It sounded re-
markably like ''I wonder.''

She studied him with a frown, just now noting the
few strands of gray above his ears and the faint red
seam of a scar along his neck. She knew nothing
about him, she realized, despite the three-hour plane
trip and one-and-a-half-hour drive from the airport.

Luke Lassiter didn't wear a ring and there had been
no mention of anyone but Aunt Clarice, so she
doubted that he was married, even though he had spo-

ken of a child. And although he talked about a number of the town's inhabitants, Luke hadn't mentioned any other family or special friends.

Jamie's happy giggles drew her from her introspection and she saw that he was seated by the coffee table, happily peeling his sandwich apart.

"Wait a minute, Jamie. I think we should go to the kitchen just in case something accidentally gets spilled." She eyed the glass of milk nervously, knowing how easily her son tipped them.

"Hogwash! Houses are for living in. If something spills, we'll clean it up. Sit down and eat up, you two. Both look like a pair of skinned beanpoles!"

"I don't think you should be talking." Luke chuckled as he plopped down onto the sofa beside his aunt. "You aren't exactly flabby yourself." He winked at Darcy. "You have to dish out as good as you get or she runs all over you," he told her, grinning. "Clarice's biggest complaint is that God took my uncle Herbert home before she was finished bossing him."

To Darcy, the comment seemed almost sacrilegious, but Clarice smiled benignly. "Man needed bossing around," she said firmly. "Couldn't find his left foot without me there to direct him. Got his money's worth when he married me, he did."

Darcy couldn't help smiling at the smug look of satisfaction on Clarice's bony face.

"You're not going to side with her, are you?" Luke complained, grabbing the dish of pickles and unloading most of it onto his plate. "It's not fair to gang up on a man like that." He turned to Jamie. "We're going to have to stick together, James, old man. You and me against the ladies."

While her son giggled his agreement, Darcy felt a jolt of shock run through her system. She dropped the half-eaten ham sandwich onto her plate, and shifted it to the table before surging to her feet.

"Why did you call him that?" She searched his dark eyes. "Have you been prying into my personal life or something?"

"I—I'm sorry," Luke stuttered, staring at her. He shook his head. "I just assumed Jamie was a nickname. It usually stands for James." He set down his plate and stood suddenly, reaching out his hand toward her shoulder. "What's wrong, Darcy?"

"Nothing." She felt stupid for her outburst. He couldn't know, could he? Nobody knew. They hadn't wanted to know back then and she sure wasn't going to bring it all up now. "I'm sorry. I guess I'm a little bit tired."

"Natural enough reaction, girl. Humanity wasn't made for streaking across the sky." Clarice poured out the tea. "Sip this. Then bed."

"I'd better go see to the chores," Luke murmured. Darcy noticed that he'd left most of the pickles and half of his sandwich on the plate. "I guess I'll see you in the morning. Good night, Jamie. Have a good sleep." He brushed his hand over the glossy dark curls and leaned down to accept the hug that the little boy offered.

Darcy met his dark apologetic glance when he straightened, and forced a smile to her lips. "Thank you for getting us here," she said solemnly. "I'm sorry if I barked at you. I guess it's just having everything come at me at once." She held out a hand. "I apologize."

Luke enfolded her hand in both of his and hung on for a long time, staring deeply into her eyes as if asking a question and searching for the answer.

"Welcome home, Darcy Simms. I hope you can remember the good times that you had here and not dwell on the bad moments. Good night." He let her hand go finally, but by that time, tiny shivers of awareness had trickled up her arm to her brain.

He was a tall, strong man who had marched into her life and confronted her with a past that she was desperately trying to avoid. But in all her twenty-three years, Darcy had never met anyone like him. The intense look in his eyes was reflected in his face as she pulled her hand away and hid it behind her back in an effort to avoid the unwanted sensations.

She *couldn't* be attracted to him. She wouldn't allow herself to be! That road only led to heartache. The men she knew only ever wanted one thing from her. And hadn't she learned the hard way that there was only pain and suffering when you followed your emotions?

"I need to get Jamie to bed," she said firmly, loudly enough for Clarice to hear. "Is there someplace where you'd prefer I put him?"

"Your old room might be best." Clarice carried the small paper bag of toys Darcy had packed up the stairs, leading the way. She put the light on in the bathroom and then bid Jamie good-night before going back downstairs.

"Come on, Love Bug," Darcy said, "this one time we'll skip brushing your teeth. You look like you're going to fall asleep in your clothes." She slid him into his pajamas without a protest, hugged him fiercely, and then waited until his dark lashes drooped closed. "I love you, Jamie." The words came out in a fierce whisper as Darcy watched him sleeping cozily in the single bed.

And then, turning her back, she went back downstairs to clean up the kitchen, steeling herself against the flood of memories that returned, stronger than ever. How many times had she washed dishes in this sink? How often had she scrubbed this floor on hands and knees in penance for some misdeed. It hurt to remember the silent meals she'd endured at the table.

She straightened her back defiantly. She was strong and competent. She would get past this guilty feeling.

Darcy Simms had not come home. She had only returned to a place where she used to live. And sooner or later the rotten reality of the past would creep up from behind and threaten to overwhelm her. She had to be strong. She had to face it. She had to beat it.

The next morning, Darcy left the cushy comfort of the renovated master suite and headed toward the kitchen with reluctance. It was the only room in the house that didn't hold memories for her and she'd been able to relax and sleep more deeply than she could ever remember. But the sun had risen long ago, streaming through the bank of east-facing windows, and she knew that it was way past time to get up.

"'Morning." Clarice's low voice came from under the sink. "Gonna snow tonight. I've got to get those everlastings in and hanging upside down in the barn if I want to save 'em for Thanksgiving. Twine's gone."

Darcy couldn't think of a thing to say to this. So

instead she asked, "Where's Jamie? I checked his room but he was gone."

"Lucas took him. Likely in the barn looking at the animals." She stood, triumphantly bearing a ball of string. "Coffee's on if you want some. If you eat it, you can get your own breakfast. Don't partake myself. Makes me logy. I'll be out back."

Darcy would have said "thanks," but Clarice disappeared out the back door in a rush, a gust of icy cold wind signaling her departure. Darcy helped herself to one of the freshly baked cinnamon rolls on the counter and poured a big mug full of coffee. There was cream in the fridge and, remembering Luke's comments from the day before, she poured some in and sipped her coffee with a grin. Colorado cream really was better!

The kitchen table was the same weathered old slab that had sat here for as long as she could remember. There were two initials carved into one of the legs. Her mother had once explained that they belonged to her grandfather, who had placed them there long ago.

"If Clarice is the one who's keeping house, she hasn't changed much of Mom's setup." Darcy glanced around the spacious area after finishing her small breakfast. She rinsed off her hands and moved quickly through the old familiar rooms of the house, noting the changes that had been made, before finally returning to the kitchen. "Evidently dusting is not Clarice's forte," Darcy said half under her breath as she trailed one finger over the top of her mother's china cabinet.

"Despise dusting." Clarice's voice crackled behind her, startling Darcy. "Be much obliged if you'd take that over. Don't like cooking much either.'' Clarice held a huge bunch of straw flowers in her arms and tilted her head toward the china cabinet. "Never did understand why folks need special dishes they only eat off of once or twice a year. Seems to me, less is more. That's what I always say."

"She does," Luke said with a chuckle as he entered the room. "About twenty times a day. Good morning, Darcy. Did you sleep well?" His eyes took in the bright red sweater that she'd chosen from among Clarice's gifts. "That's a good choice for today. It's pretty and warm."

Darcy tried not to appreciate just how handsome Luke Lassiter looked this morning.

"Where's Jamie?"

"In the barn with Ernie, our ranch hand. I never saw a child take to animals so well." Luke poured himself a cup of coffee and grabbed a roll. "He's born to ranch." As if he'd just realized what he said, his eyes opened wide and he stared at Darcy. "Sorry."

"It's all right." She shifted uncomfortably. "Are you sure he'll be okay there? He's not used to horses."

"The horses are in the pasture. Besides, Ernie will stay with him while he checks out the other animals. He'll be fine." He drank deeply from the cup, savoring the flavor. Red spots of color stood out on his cheekbones, and the ends of his fingers were white with cold. "What are you planning to do today?"

Darcy took a deep breath. "Since I'm here to settle the estate, I guess I'd better go into town and see the lawyer.'' She forced herself not to fidget. ''That should be a lot of fun.''

''Nobody going into town today,'' Clarice muttered, bundling yet another group of flowers together, her fingers nimbly tying them tightly while leaving a length of cord at the end. ''Why not get used to the place again? After all, it is your home.''

''But I'm not going to stay,'' Darcy explained carefully, wondering if the older woman was quite all there. ''I'm just here to settle the estate. Then it's back to the city for me.''

''Wonderful place, was it, this city?'' The black eyes bore straight into Darcy's. ''Everything hunky-dory there?''

''N-no.'' Darcy swallowed, opening her eyes wide at the strange expression on Clarice's face. She glanced at Luke for direction, but he looked away. ''Actually it was pretty awful. When Luke came along I was glad to leave.''

''And you need to rush back because...?'' Clarice stood straight and tall, waiting for an answer.

''I don't have to rush back. I just wanted to get things started. Find out how things stand. You know?''

''No, I don't. But I expect you want to run away again. Don't know why. No learning when you run away all the time.''

She'd never had someone coax out her private thoughts this way, Darcy decided. It was very intimidating. But she had to set the record straight.

''Look. I don't know what my parents told you, but I have never been afraid to come back here. Not really,'' she added at Clarice's knowing stare. ''It's just—" she drew in a breath of air "—it's painful for me here. I don't want to dig it all up again."

"It'll come up. Whether you want it to or not. That's life." Clarice set the last bundle into the box and carried it to the door. "Face your ghosts and move on, girl. That's the best way. You cooking lunch?" She grabbed a thick black coat from the peg and tossed it over her shoulders.

"Uh, yes. All right." It was difficult to change the subject so quickly. Darcy glanced stupidly from Clarice to Luke. "What would you like?"

"We'll eat just about anything as long as we don't have to cook it." Luke smiled, a glint of admiration in his eyes. "We've got two freezers full of beef and chickens and a whole lot of vegetables. Think you can come up with something from that?"

"Of course. I'm quite a good cook actually. I've just never had much opportunity." She checked the clock. "But I don't have a lot of time to defrost anything. Are there any eggs? I could scramble them."

"Eggs are good, healthy food. I can eat them," Clarice declared, stomping out the door and down the stairs.

"She's a bit abrupt sometimes," Luke explained from his position behind her. "I hope she didn't hurt your feelings."

"Of course not. It's just rather difficult to follow her at times, that's all." She turned to face him. "How do you work things around here?"

"I've been managing the place for a while now," he told her quietly, sinking into a chair. "Your parents trusted me to do the best I could, and the lawyers have continued that."

"There are an awful lot of horses out there." Her eyes studied the paddock across the road. "Are they all ours?"

"Not all. I started breeding some to sell. We—that is, your parents—needed the cash. It took off. Now, we've got more horses than we actually need, but I hired a man to help out a few months ago and things are working out very well. They're actually quite a profitable business." He reached across and swiped another cinnamon roll. "These are delicious."

"I thought Clarice said she didn't cook." Darcy frowned.

"She doesn't. One of the women from the church brought these. Maybe you remember her. Jalise Penner?"

"Jalise? She married Billy Penner? Oh, brother!" Darcy giggled to herself as she checked the cupboards for a tin of mushrooms. "She trailed around him from first grade on, right through high school. At least somebody around here got their dream." She laughed out loud at the thought of the tall, slim girl with the rather plain face, and the handsome boy who'd had his pick of women.

"He died two years ago," Luke murmured. "Accident."

Darcy sat down abruptly. "How awful!"

"I guess you expected that everything would stay the same, didn't you?" His voice was filled with compassion. "I'm sorry to be the bearer of bad news." His hand covered hers on the table, and, strangely, Darcy didn't mind. His touch communicated empathy and caring, comfort that she was starving for.

"Billy was the same age as me." She tried to absorb it. "He was always laughing and teasing everyone, trying to make jokes." The thought of that widetoothed grin forever gone made her shiver.

"Are you all right?"

"Yes. It's just the shock." She pulled out the eggs, onions, ham and cheese and began cracking the shells for an omelette. "Why did Clarice say I couldn't go to town?" she asked suddenly. "Surely you don't intend to keep me out here?"

"Of course not! You're not a prisoner any more than I am." He looked horrified at the thought. "It's just that a storm is on the way and I'd rather you not go. I wouldn't like to have to haul you out of a snowdrift. Can you wait?"

"Believe me, if it means that I'll be able to avoid all the nasty looks and whispered words from those busybodies, I can wait." Darcy rolled her eyes. "I suppose I just wanted to get this will thing started."

She pulled out her mother's favorite frying pan and set it on the stove. But the questions rolling around in her brain wouldn't go away. Everything was the same, and yet it was so different. Darcy turned around, hands tightening on the counter behind her. "Luke, did my parents leave a lot of money?"

His eyes narrowed. "I don't know. Why?"

"I'm not here because of the money." Darcy hurried to reassure him, noting the skeptical look on his face. "I know that there are things that need to be settled. But the place looks far better than I remember. This stove and the fridge are new. The barn looks like it was re-sided not long ago, and the machinery I saw out in the yard is not the same stuff we had five years ago." She took a breath and continued.

"My dad was as tight as they come. He wouldn't buy a thing until he absolutely had to, and then he went for the cheapest. This stove is self-cleaning, and the fridge has an ice-maker. There's an air conditioner outside and everything's been freshly painted. Why?"

"Perhaps he changed." Luke frowned at her. "People do change, you know. Even you."

"Lester Simms could never have changed that much!" She shook her head in utter disbelief. "It would take a miracle."

"Then I suppose there was a miracle because I assure you, Lester bought everything himself. He loved getting a glass of water from that fridge. He giggled like a kid when the ice cubes plopped into the glass." Luke watched as she diced the onions and ham. "The air conditioner has been a real bonus these past two summers. They were scorchers. Your mom loved to invite folks out here so they could relax in the cool. The youth group came quite often."

"The youth group?" Darcy squeaked in amazement. "But she hated all that noise. I always had to have my birthday parties outside because she said we made such a mess." Darcy laid the knife down and turned to study his placid features. "It sounds as if we're talking about different people," she whispered.

"Yeah, it does, doesn't it?" He snatched a few bits of ham and popped them into his mouth. "Maybe you didn't know them as well as you thought you did. Or maybe you just remember things differently."

That made Darcy mad. She angrily slapped his hand away from the food, then stood before him, hands on her hips, and gave him the lowdown on life in the Simms's household.

"I lived here for eighteen long, unhappy years. And during that time, I cut the potato peels as thin as possible, made do with shoes that pinched my toes because new ones were too expensive, and wore more hand-me-downs than Cinderella. Don't talk to me about the wonderful good old days." She flounced across the kitchen and pointed to a big hook.

"A flyswatter used to hang there. I can remember it even though I was only about three at the time. My parents used it on my hands when I spilled some milk on my grandmother's lace tablecloth. I never did it on purpose. But they acted as if I'd deliberately made a mess." She swallowed the pain and glared at him. "Every single thing I did was wrong. And I can never forget that!"

"I'm sorry." Luke's apology was quiet. "I'm really sorry, Darcy. I wasn't trying to make you sad or remind you of things you'd rather forget. I just thought maybe you'd—"

"You thought I'd forget all about the past, didn't you? Pretend that nothing happened, that I imagined it all." She was crying furiously now, but didn't care. "Well, I didn't imagine any of it. They were mean-spirited, unhappy people who tried to take it out on me. Maybe they liked you—I don't know. They always said a son would have been able to carry on the ranch."

"Darcy, I think I should tell you something." Luke's voice was low and ominous.

"I don't want you to tell me anything. If you liked my parents and they treated you well, I'm glad. Too bad they couldn't do the same for me." She dashed away the tears and sniffed inelegantly. "They left me with one thing," she whispered. "Just one. The assurance that I will never, never, treat my son the way they treated me."

"Darcy, I know they regretted how harsh they'd been. I think that after you left they realized that they'd been too strict with you, and since you were gone and they couldn't make amends, they tried to make it up with other people."

"They were *sorry*. They *regretted* things. Isn't that just wonderful?" Darcy sneered bitterly. "And then they repented of that sin, discussed it with Pastor Pringle, and all was well again in their narrow little world. Well, it wasn't all right for me! I'm the one who paid." The tears flowed unstopped as she leaned against the counter.

"I paid, and I paid and I paid. Because of them. And not once did they bother to find me and tell *me* that they were sorry." The pain yawned inside her brain, big and black and terrifying because this time she wasn't sure if she could stop it from enveloping her. She could hear herself sobbing and could do nothing to hold it back.

Luke's arms wrapped around her. He pulled her against his shirt, and Darcy let him. No, it was more like she couldn't stop him. She had no strength, no willpower. Nothing but an ache in her heart that wouldn't quit.

"Why did they have to go, without saying anything, without contacting me? Without even seeing Jamie. Why, Luke?" She scrunched his shirt up under her fingers and squeezed, willing the hurt away. "The youth group, you, Clarice. They gave to everyone but me. And I was their daughter, Luke. Their own *daughter.''* She felt his hand move soothingly up her back as his other brushed over her hair.

"It's all right. Let it out. You've carried this for far too long." He murmured soothing phrases as the slide show in her head continued flashing images from the past.

"Why couldn't they have said, just once, that they loved me? That they liked me just because I was me? Why did they have to always keep trying to make me into someone else?"

"I don't know. I don't know." His chin rested on her head, and she relaxed against him weakly.

"I tried to do what they wanted. I tried to be who they needed. But I'm me, Luke. Me, *Darcy.* I was neither the little china-doll daughter nor the in-control son that they wanted. But I wasn't all bad! I *wasn't,* Luke."

"I know. The three of you just got off the track somewhere and couldn't get back on. If only you'd come back home, Darcy. Maybe then you and your parents could have straightened things out."

Darcy yanked herself out of his arms, red-hot fury chasing away all the other emotions that clawed at her. "Come back?" she gasped. "To what? Being told how much of a disappointment I was because I'd had a child out of wedlock? Come back to the sad, commiserating glances between my parents and their friends that the local bad girl had taken that final step to perdition?" She laughed harshly.

"Yeah, that would have been a barrel of laughs, Luke. And Jamie would have grown up feeling like he was a mistake, a problem, something to be avoided." She shook her head vehemently. "No, thank you very much!"

"Darcy, they wouldn't have thought that! They would have loved him."

"They couldn't love me," she told him bitterly. "And I was their own flesh and blood."

"But you don't know the whole story." He looked pained, Darcy decided. As if there was something he wanted to say but couldn't find the words. "If you knew—"

"If I knew, I would have stayed exactly where I was." Darcy turned back to the counter and tossed the ham and onion into the egg mixture determinedly. "You can never go back, Luke. Isn't that the saying?" She smiled grimly. "Actually, I think it's a good one. I don't want to go back and live through that horrible time. I want to move on."

"To what?" He asked it quietly, his eyes sad.

"To something better. I have a wonderful son. I want to show him the lovely things in the world. And that doesn't include any of my memories of this place." She turned on the burner and began making the omelette. "I'll stay here until things are settled, but then I'm leaving."

"And the ranch?"

"Will have to be sold to pay off their debts. I don't care about the money. Really I don't." She faced him defiantly.

"You mean you don't like sleeping safely in a warm bed with a full stomach and not having to worry whether someone will smash down the door, shoot off a gun or worse?"

He sounded angry and that irritated Darcy. Why couldn't he understand?

"Oh, I like it all right," she told him. "I'm not crazy, you know. I want all the best things for my son."

"But?"

"But the best things aren't always the things money can buy. And to tell you the truth, some things just plain cost too much. If anybody knows that, it's me."

The door closed softly several moments later, and she turned to watch as Luke crossed the yard. Clarice and Jamie were bent over a bale, earnestly discussing something. They waved at Luke, and Clarice nodded at something he said. Jamie's little face was red and glowing with good health as he scampered over to the big man who leaned down and scooped him up, hugging the little body close.

Darcy turned away to butter the toast and flip the eggs. She didn't know why, but she was certain that Jamie was perfectly safe with Luke and Clarice. They would encourage him to check things out, but make sure that he didn't get hurt. She'd seen the glow in Luke's eyes yesterday when he'd spoken to her son. The big, solid cowboy had answered every question as patiently as any father.

"Why didn't You give *me* a father like that?" Darcy glared at the ceiling, thinking of a God who would stand by while children suffered. "Why couldn't You give me parents that loved me like the other kids' parents did?"

Quick as a wink, the answer raced through her mind.

You didn't deserve that kind of love. You lied, cheated, stole and hurt people. How could anyone love you?

Heartsick and weary, Darcy tugged open the door and called the others to lunch. Why, oh, why had she ever come back?

Chapter Four

"Come on, son. Let's walk over here." One week later and Darcy was still nervous about being home.

Darcy grabbed Jamie's hand and hurried down the street, anxious to get to the lawyer's office and then run back to the safety of the farm. Funny, thinking the farm was safer than the town. Neither one had been exactly a haven of peace five years ago.

The hardest thing was listening to the speculation that whispered behind her.

"...Isn't that the Simms girl...?"

"...That's her kid? Cute little guy. Looks a little like Martha...."

"...Wonder how old he is...?"

They'd know soon enough, so there really wasn't any point in trying to hide the facts of his conception. But she had no intention of having his name dragged through the mud either, Darcy decided grimly.

"Hello, Darcy. Back in town, I see." Marietta Follensbee stood peering down at Jamie. "Is he yours?" she asked with a grim tightening of her lips.

"Yes. This is my son, Jamie, Mrs. Follensbee."

"Hmm. Looks a might peaked." Marietta reached out and pinched the skin of Jamie's cheek between two gnarled fingers. "Needs some good outside work and a few early nights to toughen him up, I'll warrant."

"He's only four! And Jamie is not *sickly* at all. Good day!" Darcy marched down the street to the drugstore as the knot of tension tightened its band around her forehead.

"Darcy." Elroy Spiggot stood behind the counter in his white jacket—the same one he'd worn for the past thirty years. His spectacles perched on the end of his nose and he peered through them haughtily.

"Hi, Mr. Spiggot. How are you and your wife doing?" Darcy did her best to sound interested in the two elderly hypochondriacs.

"Mrs. Spiggot died three years back. Food poisoning, it was. I don't suppose you knew, since you never made the effort to come back and see your own folks." There was condemnation clear and present in those tones, and Darcy shrank inwardly from the malice that glowed in the pharmacist's eyes. "Too ashamed of yourself, I expect. Be sure your sins will find you out, the Good Book says. I reckon they did just that." His gaze slid to Jamie, one eyebrow tilted meaningfully.

"No, Mr. Spiggot." Darcy enunciated each word clearly and precisely. "I was not ashamed to come back. I didn't want to return to a place where there were so many people waiting to take God's place as judge and jury. I apologized to you for stealing that candy bar and I worked for you without pay for two weeks as my parents wished. The debt is paid."

She wasn't going to go away silently, Darcy decided bitterly. They wouldn't intimidate her as they had in the past.

"But just for your information, this is my *son*. His name is Jamie. He's a wonderful little boy who is innocent of anything I might have done." She turned toward the door, tugging Jamie along. "I think I can get whatever I need in the city, Mr. Spiggot. No need to bother yourself." She pulled open the door. "And, believe it or not, I am very sorry to hear about your wife. As, I'm sure, you were sorry to hear about my parents. Goodbye."

"We didn't get nothing, Mommy. You said we had to get something." Jamie stood frowning up at her, his little face curious.

Darcy sucked in a deep breath and let it out slowly between her teeth. That had been a tough one. And there was worse to come, if she knew the good citizens of Raven's Rest. And she did!

"No, sunshine boy, we didn't get anything. I decided it was too cold in there and I didn't want to stay very long." Which was a major understatement, Darcy admitted to herself grimly. But there was no way she wanted to color Jamie's view of the town with her own bad experiences.

"I didn't think it was cold in there. I thought it was hot! But I didn't like that man, Mommy. He looked too grumpy."

Darcy burst out laughing at this very accurate assessment, and hugged Jamie close. "I love you, sweetie. More and more every day."

Jamie's cold little lips brushed against her cheek as his chubby arms tugged against her neck. "I love you, too, Mommy. This much." And he squeezed for all he was worth.

"Let's go get some new crayons from that store over there." Darcy urged him across the street, but when they reached the other side, she was surprised to see Mr. Spiggot still standing in the window of his store, watching them. She deliberately turned her back on him.

"I think we need some really bright colors," she murmured to Jamie. "Something to brighten up this place a little."

"Still trying to change things, eh, Darce?" asked the tall man who stood before her.

"Todd? Todd Barlow?" Darcy studied the bearded face, frowning.

"Yeah, it's me."

"You sure look different. Kind of...older, I guess." It wasn't exactly complimentary, but the man in the brown button-down suit with the color-coordinated tie and shiny wingtips was a far cry from the blue-jeaned hoodlum she'd chummed around with years ago. "Are you still living here?"

"Yes, of course I live here. I run the store with my father. I'm married to Sara Higgins." He brushed a hand over his mustache with a self-satisfied smile that made Darcy only too aware that Todd felt superior to her.

"You and Sara? Well, congratulations. I didn't realize you even liked each other."

"Of course we like each other. We're married. Sara teaches at the school. In fact she's the vice-principal." Todd glanced down condescendingly.

"Oh, that's nice. You were dating Annette when I left. Oh, this is my son, Jamie. Jamie, this is an old friend of mine from when I lived here."

Jamie thrust out his hand. "Hello."

"Hello." Todd's fingers barely brushed the child's before he thrust his briefcase into his other hand. "Did your husband come too, or are you just here long enough to settle up the ranch with Luke?"

"I'm not married, Todd. And no, Jamie and I haven't made any plans. We're taking things one day at a time."

"Yes, I remember that about you." Todd glanced at his watch. "You never did like to be scheduled into anything, did you, Darce? Always the rebel. Well, times change, and we all get older. You need to think about the future now, just like the rest of us. We can't stay children forever, Darcy. It's time to be an adult." He shifted impatiently.

"Yes, I suppose I should take a leaf out of your book, Todd. You always were the one who planned out our schemes so well. For years I wondered how the rest of us always got caught while you managed to make a getaway. Must have been that planning you did so carefully, right?" Darcy stared up at him, wide-eyed and innocent, watching in satisfaction as his face flushed a deep, dark red.

"Maybe I'll go and see the lawyer, while I'm here. Might as well get on with disposing of things so I can move on. You know, Todd—plan for the future."

"Yes, well..." Todd edged around her carefully.

"I suppose I'll be seeing you at the adult fellowship meeting on Saturday night, then."

"Oh, I don't think so. I'm not too sure that I fit in around here anymore. Do you?" Darcy didn't wait for his words, but turned and walked into the store with Jamie skipping along behind. "Here we go, Jamie. Nice bright crayons, lots of them. How about this?"

She swallowed her anger and frustration and tried to forget the contempt in those silky-smooth tones. She wouldn't be suckered into Todd's petty one-upmanship games—not this time.

She paid for the crayons out of her few remaining funds and, with a smile, handed Jamie the bag. As they walked along the street searching for the lawyer's office, Darcy focused on the future. Her future. One far away from here.

Her mind was so intent on her mission that she didn't even see Luke heading toward them until she bumped right into him.

"Darcy? I didn't know you were coming into town today. I could have given you a lift after I finished the chores." Luke carefully set her away from him with a grin. When she didn't return it, he stood on the curb frowning. "Is everything all right?"

"No," she told him through clenched teeth. "Everything is not all right. I feel like I'm making a spectacle of myself standing here, even *being* here, in this one-horse town!"

"How did you get into town?" He picked up Jamie's mittens and handed them back to the child.

"Clarice came in for her ladies' meeting, and I thought maybe I could get some business done. The lawyer's offices have moved." She glanced around. "A lot seems to have changed in Raven's Rest."

"I did tell you that, remember?" His face creased in that grin that lifted the corners of his eyes. Darcy couldn't help but smile back.

"Yes, you did. Thanks. And I told you that a lot had stayed the same, too." She spared a glance over her shoulder to check for Mr. Spiggot's presence. "I was also right. Now, if you can just tell me where Mr. Pettigrew's office is currently located, I can go see him. I assume he is still my parents' lawyer?"

"Hey, Lucas! Who's the babe? Pretty cool!" A pair of teenaged boys winked at Luke as they gazed at Darcy.

"Randy. Caleb. No school today?" Luke was cool but friendly, his fingers tightening fractionally on Darcy's elbow.

"Yeah, there's school. There's always school." Caleb, at least, wasn't intimidated by Luke's warning glance. "You gonna introduce us, man?"

"This is Darcy Simms. And her son, Jamie."

"You're kidding? Martha's long-lost daughter? Pleased to meet you!" Caleb shook her hand as if he'd waited a lifetime, and would have kept on except that Darcy finally pulled her stiffened fingers away.

"All right! So you did it, eh, Luke? Lester'd be happy as a clam that you brought her back."

"You knew my parents?" Darcy was stunned at the looks on the faces of these two less-than-handsome youths. Neither one seemed exactly clean. Their stringy long hair, ragged jeans and gold earrings were about as acceptable in stodgy old Raven's Rest as leaving your garbage on the street.

"Sure we knew 'em," Randy told her. "We spent more hours out at their place than anybody else's in town. Lester was helping us build a stock car. It must still be there." He looked to Luke for confirmation.

"And your mom was the best listener we ever had. She's the one who got me to talk to my dad about building the car. I don't think he would have coughed up that cash except that Martha got Lester to match my dad, dollar for dollar."

Darcy couldn't believe it. They were talking about *her* parents? The Martha and Lester Simms who had refused to take her to the local fair because it might corrupt her?

"How could you leave such a great place?" Randy wanted to know. "If I had parents like that, I'd stay home all the time!"

"Yeah, me too. You didn't even write at Christmas. Martha told me one day when I was sitting with her. She felt bad about that." Caleb's eyes were filled with curiosity.

"They weren't always like that," Darcy burst out, unable to listen to any more of this. "I had perfectly good reasons for leaving home, you know. And my parents were two of the best." Darcy clamped her lips closed.

She shouldn't have said it. She should have shut up about the past, kept it bottled up inside rather than spilling out the pain of her childhood all over these kids. They didn't need to have their memories tainted with her ugly past.

"I'm sorry, boys." Luke broke into the conversation. "Darcy hasn't been back all that long and she just found out recently that her mom and dad passed away. Maybe you could talk to her about it all another day.''

"Sure, man." Randy frowned at her. "I didn't mean to upset you. Sometimes people say things that hurt other people and they don't even realize it. I'm sorry if that's what we've done."

"It's all right. It's not your fault. I shouldn't have said anything." Darcy clutched Jamie's hand a little more tightly and stepped off the curb. "Goodbye."

Luke stayed behind talking quietly to Randy and Caleb.

Darcy didn't know what they said, but she could feel the scrutiny of their eyes from a block away, where she stopped to catch her breath. Miraculously, Percy Pettigrew's office was right in front of her. Darcy shoved the door open and went inside, pulling Jamie along.

"Hi, I'm Darcy Simms. I wonder if I could speak to Mr. Pettigrew. I believe he was the lawyer for my parents' estate."

"Darcy Simms, as I live and breathe!" A bustling woman of about fifty-five whipped out from behind the desk and rushed forward. "How are you, dear?" she asked, enveloping Darcy in a perfumed hug. "You've certainly lost weight since high school."

"Uh, yes. I suppose so." Darcy studied the stylish blonde for several moments. No enlightenment came. "I'm sorry, I…"

"You don't remember me?" The blonde laughed in a twitter that set her dangling earrings bouncing against her cheeks. "Of course you don't. I myself weighed a lot more in those not-so-happy days. And of course, I was a brunette. I'm Mary Pickens, Darcy.''

She couldn't help it. Darcy stared at the woman who had once embarrassed her so thoroughly that she had doubted she would ever live through it all.

"Hello," she managed in a choked voice.

"It's all right." Mary smiled. "I know I've changed quite a lot. Good thing, too. I was pretty pathetic before."

Darcy didn't know what to say so she kept quiet, waiting for the slam she knew would come. Mary had never chosen her words with regard to the other person. Just one more thing that hadn't changed.

"Is this your son?" Mary asked, glancing down at Jamie. "He's almost the same age as Annette's Jordan. Do you remember Annette?"

Who could forget the bossy manipulative Annette? Darcy wanted to demand.

"No, I see you don't." Mary sighed. "I wish some of us could forget the Annette from the past. She could use a little forgiveness."

"Is she ill?" Darcy asked perfunctorily, not really wanting to know how the town's spoiled brat was faring.

"No, she's healthy enough. She's just trying to sort out some problems in her life and it's not easy. I should know. I helped create some of them by forcing her to be someone she isn't. Please sit down, Darcy."

They sat in the pretty plum chairs. Mary handed Jamie a coloring book, and he took out his new crayons, immediately engrossed in the cartoon characters.

"You know, I've waited such a long time to do

this," Mary murmured, tears forming at the corners of her eyes. "I should have the words memorized."

"Waited to do what?" Darcy stared at the woman. What was this all about?

"I've been wanting to apologize to you. For saying those things after the prom that year. It was none of my business and I should never have listened to gossip. I wanted Josiah for my Annette, you see. He was the best-looking boy in your group, and Annette claimed she was in love with him." Mary sighed.

"I got myself all worked up when the two of you started dating, and that night I'm afraid I lashed out. If I could take those horrible words back, Darcy, I would. Please believe me."

Time rolled back and it was six years ago… Josiah Pringle loved her and she was the luckiest girl in the world. They'd spent every dance holding each other, relishing the special time together.

Until Mary Pickens had ruined everything by telling the whole gymnasium that she had seen Darcy and Josiah necking on Lookout Point. Those awful, hateful words had stripped Darcy of every bit of joy, and left her standing, empty and lost, as her school chums looked on.

Her parents had been horrified as they'd driven her home, refusing to listen to anything she tried to say. Thanks to Mary Pickens, Darcy's reputation as the town bad girl had solidified in everyone's minds, but especially in her parents' minds.

"Can you ever forgive me?" Mary's pale green eyes were full of tears. "I know my words were what sent you down the path to self-destruction. I was the one who tore you apart. I could see how much you loved that kid, yet I went ahead and did it anyway—took away the most wonderful thing in your young life. I'm sorry, Darcy. More sorry than I can ever say.''

"It doesn't matter," Darcy mumbled, clenching her purse in her hands as she stared at her feet. "It's in the past."

"It matters to me. I needed to apologize. I told your parents what I'd done, too. Last year. I needed to clear my conscience."

"You told them that you'd made it all up? That Josiah and I weren't anywhere near Lookout Point that night?" Darcy frowned. "What did they say?"

"Not much. They thanked me for telling them and said they'd have to pray for forgiveness themselves." She shrugged. "I'm sorry I didn't do it years ago. My only explanation is that I wanted the best for Annette. I guess every mother does."

"You'd think so, wouldn't you?" Darcy stared down at Jamie's glossy bright head. How much, she wondered idly, would Martha have been willing to forgive, knowing that Jamie was on the way six months later? And that he was a product of exactly the type of scene Mary had described to the entire town?

"So were you needing something specific?" Mary's face was a question. "I know you aren't here to see little old me."

"Actually, it's really nice to see you again." And to know that not everything around this town has stayed the same, Darcy added mentally. "But I was hoping to see Mr. Pettigrew. I want to get some of the details about the ranch sorted out. I'm sure Luke and Clarice would like to move on with their lives also.''

''Move on?'' Mary had a strange look on her face. ''Oh, you mean figure out how to handle things from hereon in? Yes, I can see that you would need to set that up. But I'm afraid Percy's out of the office for a while. He's had some heart trouble and is in Denver right now. I'm not sure just when he'll be back.''

''I'm sorry to hear that. I hope it's not serious.'' Darcy felt her heart sink to her shoes. So, no quick flight. She was going to be stuck here for a while, trying to settle everything. Well, at least the ranch was far enough out of town that she wouldn't have to endure all the gossips.

''I don't think so. He always calls these trips his 'tune-ups.' He has a pacemaker, you know, and I guess from time to time it requires adjusting.''

''Then perhaps you could give me a call when he returns. I'd really like to get everything ironed out as soon as possible.'' Darcy gathered up Jamie's crayons and helped him on with his jacket. ''It's a little hard to know just what to do next.''

''Everything has been set up quite well, Darcy. Please don't worry about a thing. Martha and Lester knew what they wanted, and Percy's very good at making sure it's ironclad. Just have patience.'' She patted Darcy's hand sympathetically. ''So easy to say and so hard to do. Believe me, my dear, I know all about it. But the Lord is in control. He'll deal with it all.''

''Thanks, Mary. I'll try not to hassle you too often.''

''Nonsense! If you need anything, I'm right here.

Just let me know. I'm glad you came back, Darcy. I've missed your wonderful happy spirit." Mary's voice was soft with—what? Compassion? Caring?

Darcy could hardly believe this was the same woman who had caused her so much pain. And yet, if Mary got the chance, wasn't it possible that she might do it all again? It was better for Darcy and Jamie if she didn't give in to her need for a friend. Not in Raven's Rest, at least.

"Thanks again. 'Bye, Mary." As she walked out of the office, and back to the seniors' hall, Darcy shook her head in wonder. It had been a very strange day. But the true test was still to come.

"Hello, you two." Clarice beamed as Darcy led Jamie into the huge room. Every elderly woman in the town was there and every one of their nosy probing eyes focused on her.

"Hi, Clarice. I'm sorry. I thought you would be finished." Darcy tried to ignore the curious stares and barely controlled herself from hiding Jamie's scared face in the folds of her jacket.

"Almost done. Deciding on a project. I vote for the boxes." She leaned over toward Darcy, who'd seated herself on a hard wooden chair nearby. "Those boxes. Some kind of purse, they call it. Never remember."

"It's *Samaritan's Purse*," Edilia Weatherby sighed. "I've told you three times. And it's a very worthwhile Christmas gift idea for children who are needy."

"It sounds lovely," Darcy murmured, peering into the display box with interest. There was an assortment of pencils and erasers, a writing pad, some toothpaste, a roll of hard candies and three windup toys. "What ages are they for?"

"You can choose 'em," Clarice was muttering as she gathered up several of the boxes into her arms. "If you don't want to do it, I'll send these myself."

"Now, Clarice," Harriet Heppworth chided. "We didn't say we didn't *want* to do them. We haven't really decided. We have to take a vote. All in favor?" About fifteen of the twenty-five hands went up.

"Carried," Clarice announced in smug satisfaction. "Move adjournment."

"Really, Clarice! Must you rush us so? We want to have coffee yet, you know." Edilia preened. "I brought a cheesecake that's simply to die for—triple chocolate," she announced proudly.

"Can't eat chocolate. Too rich. Sure wouldn't die for it!" Clarice dropped the boxes into a cavernous bag she'd produced. "Coffee's okay, though."

"Do I take it we're adjourned then?" Harriet glanced from one nodding head to the next. "I do wish we could do things in an orderly fashion, ladies. Next meeting in two weeks." She smacked the home-made gavel against the table and watched morosely as the ladies who were serving shuffled over to the counter.

Darcy took it all in with a smile as she served some cake to Jamie and helped herself. She'd seen the same thing hundreds of times when her mother had been alive and she'd called in after school. The ladies of the community had good hearts for the needy souls who lived outside Raven's Rest. It was the ones inside the town boundaries that they had problems with.

"Darcy! How are you, dear? And this is your son, is it? He looks just like Jo—"

"Esther! Come and serve the tea."

"How old is the boy, Darcy?"

"He's four and his name is Jamie." As I'm sure you already know, she added mentally. "He'll be five in January." She said it stiffly, scrutinizing the faces carefully.

"I expect it will be good for the child to be around Luke," Harriet murmured with a sly smile. "He's already had some practice at fathering, and I'm sure little Jamie here could do worse. Him being without a father and all."

"Luke needs a new family," Olivia Hernsburg added, nodding thoughtfully. "He's been alone long enough now. It's time for him to look to the future. Especially with the ranch and all."

There was a long drawn-out silence then that made Darcy stare. It was as if everyone were holding their breaths, waiting for her to say something. But what could she say? She had no idea what they were talking about.

"I expect that's why you sent Luke to fetch her, isn't it, Clarice? Kind of kills two birds with one stone, if you know what I mean?" Edilia winked at everyone in general.

"Stuff's okay," Clarice butted in, holding her fork aloft from the piece of cheesecake she was tasting. "Bit too much salt, though."

"As if you'd know. You never bake anything to bring to these meetings. It's always from the bakery!" Edilia smirked nastily, and Darcy knew she didn't like the comment about her prize cheesecake. But in actual fact, Darcy agreed with Clarice. There *was* too much salt. And the chocolate was grainy.

"Bringing something next time," Clarice muttered, shoving away the rich, almost untouched dessert.

"Like what?"

"Don't know yet. Whatever strikes my fancy." Clarice brazenly outstared them all, and Darcy wanted to cheer her on.

"You're just trying to get them off the track, Clarice," Esther chirped into the conversation. "And it won't work. I know why she's so suddenly back here, rubbing our noses in her past. Darcy doesn't have a father for her child. You know it as well as anyone in this room. If she's telling the truth now, she was pregnant when she left here." Esther smoothed down her coiffed silver hair with a graceful hand that glittered with rings. Her eyes were hard with disdain.

"But I can hardly imagine that Luke Lassiter is prepared to take another man's leavings just to get his hands on all of that ranch. That seems a bit too much of a sacrifice, even for a kindly man like him."

Darcy had always wondered what nonplused meant. As the blood drained from her face and twenty-five nosey parkers stared at her, she suddenly knew. She couldn't believe anyone had actually said the words out loud. Even here in Raven's Rest, people usually still pretended to have manners.

Thousands of thoughts poured through Darcy's mind, and none of them, not one, was kind. Fury boiled like acid in her veins, eating her up with anger and indignation. How dare they!

"I didn't come back to find a father for Jamie, if that's what you're implying, Mrs. Fairfield. And I highly doubt that Luke suddenly feels the need for a family to replace the one he lost.'' She swallowed her tears and strove to strengthen her voice, determined that none of these vicious old biddies would see her cry.

"In fact, there is really only one reason why I would come back to this hotbed of gossip and discontent, where people spread scandal for the fun of it.'' She bundled up Jamie, wiped his face on a napkin, and slipped on her own jacket, her eyes meeting Clarice's. Luke's elderly aunt smiled and nodded approvingly, and Darcy straightened as a rush of courage bolstered her.

"I came back because my parents died and I owed it to them to see that their last wishes are carried out. But I don't owe anything to you. Neither does my son.'' She snatched up the purse that Clarice had given her and marched across the room.

"Neither does Luke,'' she snapped and swung out the door.

Behind her, Clarice was speaking. Darcy stopped just long enough to hear her words to the startled ladies who sat with their mouths hanging open.

"God has forgiven some of you even *your* terrible sins,'' Clarice said in a clear clipped voice that conveyed her displeasure. "Ought to think about that.'' There was a dearth of noise in the hall as she stomped across the room, boxes in tow.

"Idle tongues—'' she muttered, tossing everything into the trunk and slamming it closed. Her eyes sparkled like black bits of onyx as they met Darcy's.

"—Most dangerous member in the whole human body. Bad news in this town."

Darcy couldn't stop the laugh that burst from her throat as they drove away.

Chapter Five

Luke smiled as he watched Darcy chase a squealing Jamie through the drifts of snow. Just this once he allowed himself to enjoy the scene without harking back to the past. Maybe he really was healing. Maybe he *would* be able to face life without his family beside him. But he would never forget them.

"Nice," Clarice murmured from behind him. "'Bout time the girl laughed. Far too serious."

"Yes, she is," Luke agreed, sipping his afternoon coffee. "And thank you for making her feel welcome. It took a couple of weeks but she's thawing."

"She's hurting." Clarice stated the fact in a loud clear voice. "Runs herself ragged to stop thinking. Don't expect she'll stay around long."

"She's going to have to stay a little longer. Percy's stay in Denver has been extended. I don't know if it's his heart." Luke's glance moved back to the window. "She won't like it."

"Needs to get involved in something away from

here." Clarice studied him seriously. "Got any ideas?"

Luke shook his head. "I tried to suggest the local ladies' group or maybe helping out with the choir, but she blew me off with some drivel about spending more time with Jamie. As if she doesn't spend all day with him now."

"Needs time with him," Clarice remarked sagely, nodding her gray head. "Probably missed a lot of his babyhood, what with working and all. I could give Lester Simms a good tongue-lashing right about now!"

Luke leaned back from her waving fingers. Aunt Clarice in this mood was not to be trifled with. Still, he'd like to know what she was talking about. "Why?" He asked it carefully.

"Man was a niddling," she told him shortly.

"A what?" He frowned, trying to remember if he'd heard this particular descriptive before.

"A niddling. Pay attention, boy. Don't you know the English language?" She took a huge gulp of coffee. "Means he was a fool not to see the potential in that girl."

"Oh." Luke decided to look the word up later, once Clarice went to bed. He was pretty sure he wouldn't find it in any dictionary. Clarice's words often weren't. "Maybe—" he shrugged, unwilling to get into that discussion again "—but that was then and this is now. What are we going to do about it?"

"Get her busy, involved with somebody besides those old tabbies that harangued her last week," Clarice informed him as she marched to the door to call the others in. "Less time to dwell on the past, more time to think about the future."

And so it was that Luke found himself reading stories to Jamie in front of the fire that night while Clarice and Darcy buried themselves in the basement.

"Need your help," Clarice mumbled as she moved past the cold storage room with its jars of canned preserves safely stowed away. She opened the door at the end of the hall and flicked on a light, illuminating a small room lined with plastic. A huge sturdy workroom stood at one end, and above it shelves full of dried or drying pottery pieces.

"You're a potter?" Darcy gaped in amazement. Clay vessels of every shape and description sat on the shelves, on the tables, even on the floor. "I didn't realize."

"Lots don't." Clarice donned a big denim apron. "I have a class with the third graders tomorrow, and I figured you could help."

"Me? I don't know anything about pottery!" Darcy protested, running a curious finger down the smooth, wet clay that Clarice uncovered.

"You can learn, can't you?" Clarice pulled a wire from her pocket. She hung onto the two wooden ends and pulled the hair-thin wire through the clay in a deft motion that left a piece free at the top.

"I don't know." Darcy pulled off a small piece from the larger hunk and squeezed gently. "I don't think I'm the type. I never did well in art class."

"Clay isn't just a piece of delicate white paper that you have to throw out if you mess up," Clarice snorted inelegantly. "It's clay. If you don't like what you've made, you squash it up and start again. Nothing as forgiving as clay. 'Cept maybe the Lord.'' She seemed to think about that for a moment.

"What are you going to demonstrate?" Darcy watched as the other woman kneaded the huge lump of clay into a sort of fat cone shape with the swift action of her hands. "It looks like you're working bread dough."

"Same idea," Clarice nodded. "Have to get the air bubbles out." Apparently she wasn't satisfied that they were all gone, for she lifted the great grayish hunk in both of her small hands and slammed the mass onto the table. "Good. Now, flatten it."

Darcy wasn't sure whether the woman was talking to herself or to her assistant, so she stayed where she was and watched. In a matter of moments Clarice had a section of the clay flattened out on the table and was rolling an old wooden rolling pin over it.

"Your parents let me set this studio up down here after Luke and I moved in," she told Darcy. "I've been working with this stuff for so long, I just couldn't give it up now."

"Oh." There had been so many surprises lately that Darcy let this one go. "Why are there plastic sheets covering the walls?" Darcy studied the room curiously. "It looks like there's clay on them, but you couldn't make that much mess."

Clarice let out a cackle of mirth, her widow's peak giving her a wicked, witchlike look in the glaring overhead light. "You think not? Missy, when I get my wheel going, there's clay flying all over the place." She flipped the sheet of clay over as deftly as Darcy's mother had once flipped a pie crust.

"I thought of showing them how to make a box," she explained as her fingers moved nimbly. "The girls could make theirs into gifts for Christmas if they wanted. The boys, too. Or they could build coil pots." As she spoke, Clarice rolled out long rolls of clay and began laying them on the slab with a dab of water along the joining edge. Within seconds, she had the beginnings of a large box.

"Why don't you just flatten more clay and cut out the sides? It would sure be quicker."

"Quicker isn't necessarily better when you're working with clay." Clarice grunted as she worked. "Kind of like life, too, I guess. Patience is a virtue."

"You mean you can't do it?" Darcy curiously studied the rapidly building box.

"Sure you can do it. But you have to wait until the sides are dry enough to stand up by themselves and not too dry so that they'll crack. Touchy business. Too difficult for twenty-five third graders to tackle all at once." She glanced up to wink at Darcy. "Always reminds me of the way God has to carefully work in our lives or we get toppled because we're not prepared for His mighty touch."

"Can I try coiling something?" Clarice motioned to the rolls of clay, and Darcy picked one up, twirling it carefully around her finger. "What do I do?"

"Dip your finger in the water and then moisten the two seams," Clarice explained as she worked. "Push them together a little bit, too. Otherwise you end up with a perfectly shaped pile of coils that usually comes apart."

"Are you supposed to preserve the shape of the coils or make it look smooth, so you can't tell where the joins are?'' Darcy frowned at the tilting form in front of her.

"You are the potter, Darcy. You have to make your own choices and then work to carry them out.'' Clarice stopped working, her green eyes shining. Her words were soft but full of meaning as she stared at Darcy. "It's exactly the same as life. You get a picture of what you want your life to be about and then you work to create that.''

Darcy thought about it while she fiddled with her pot, placing coil upon coil. Clarice was mostly silent and Darcy found the words that she'd just said rolling around her brain.

Get a picture of what you want your life to be about...

Well, she'd had that for a long time, she decided, adding more water to the clay and smoothing away the bumps of each coil until the outside of the pot was smooth and glossy. She wanted her life to be about love and caring—the things she had missed out on.

"So how are you going to make the picture happen?'' Clarice's voice abruptly broke the spell, and Darcy jerked, knocking over her pot. "Oh, sorry,'' the other woman muttered, reaching over to try to right it.

"It won't hold its shape now,'' Darcy muttered in frustration, her fingers clumsy against the wet, slippery surface.

"Too much water. Too much of anything weakens a person just like it does a pot. Too much trouble, a body can't abide it. Not enough and he gets complacent.'' Clarice took out her wire. "Just like a pot. Too much water and it sags away into nothingness." With a flick of her wrist, she cut through the pot from top to bottom leaving two halves standing on the table.

"Why did you do that?" Darcy asked, more curious than angry at the ruination of her creation.

"A good potter wants his work to look just as good inside as it does outside," Clarice muttered, pointing one bony finger at the obvious lumps and bumps. "It would have leaked here eventually," she explained. "Or fallen apart in the kiln. It's not strong enough, not connected with the rest."

"And I suppose you're going to say that it's the same with life," Darcy muttered in frustration, squeezing the squishy mess between her fingers. "If people don't stay connected, we lose our solidarity." She looked at Clarice defiantly. "Right?"

"Not just my opinion, either," Clarice told her happily. "Says so in The Book." She scooped up Darcy's sloppy mess and massaged it in with her own leftover bits.

"If it's no good for anything, why don't you just throw it out?" Darcy washed her hands in the big sink, grateful for the warm flow of water after the cool clay.

"Hardly ever throw clay out," Clarice informed her. "Mix it in with some more, let it dry, add some water. Whatever it needs, it can usually be used again. It's only after you fire it that clay can't be changed."

"What about when it's dried out? Say someone neglected it, left it out in the elements?" Darcy challenged her deliberately, meeting that all-knowing look. "What about then?"

"It can still be used. But it's got to go through a

lot of painful processes first to make it serviceable again.'' She stopped what she was doing and met Darcy's stare head-on. Darcy knew that, once again, she wasn't talking just about the clay.

''And I suppose you think that's what I have to do. Mull over the past some more.''

''Nope.'' Clarice covered her box with a bit of plastic and began straightening the counter.

''Then what *do* you think?'' Darcy prodded, growing irritated with the conversation.

''Think you've thought enough about the past. Time to get on with your life. Meet it on the chin and keep going.''

''And you think I should do this how? By immediately joining a bunch of gossiping ladies' groups? As if they'd let me! Or maybe I should go to church on Sunday and sit in the front row so I could beg everyone's forgiveness for not being here when my parents died.'' Darcy stomped upstairs behind the older woman and followed her into the kitchen, her anger growing. ''I think you're forgetting just who's in the wrong here.''

''Does it really matter anymore?'' Clarice poured out two cups of coffee and set them down on the table, adding a plate of cookies before she dropped down on a chair. ''What difference does it make?'' she asked in a kind voice. ''The past is past, done, over with. You can't change it. God doesn't expect you to.''

Darcy frowned at the repeated reference to some heavenly interest in her mundane life. ''So what does He expect?''

''He expects you to use this new opportunity He's

given you." Clarice's black eyes shone back at her. "He expects you to deal with the past and move on. Or are you going to let it poison your mind forever?"

"My mind isn't poisoned," Darcy hotly denied. "But I can't just ignore everything that happened!" She gestured at the familiar room. "Being here, in this house, reminds me of it all over again."

"I imagine it does. So face it," Clarice challenged. "Look it square in the eye and say, 'Yes, I got a rough deal. Some of it I deserved, and some of it I didn't. But it's over now and I'm moving on.' Can you do that?" The words were harsh, but her voice was soft and full of compassion.

"You think I deserved to be treated the way I was?" Darcy demanded, her cheeks warm with anger. She couldn't believe it. Clarice was just like everyone else in this hick town, blaming her for all the problems. It was the past all over again.

"Oh, Darcy!" The bony hand reached across to enfold hers, squeezing gently when Darcy would have pulled away. "I'm not saying you should have been treated the way you were. And I'm not denying that this treatment caused a lot of problems in your life. What I am saying is that we humans are often the authors of our own misfortune. Some of the things you did added to your problems. Am I right?"

In all fairness, Darcy knew she couldn't deny it. She had accepted everyone else's opinion of her and played on that because she had half believed it herself.

"The wild parties, staying out so late, playing those rather nasty tricks—didn't they all contribute to the reputation you say you didn't deserve?"

"I wanted to have friends," Darcy muttered, loath to recall those painful years. "I just wanted to fit in, to belong."

"And the troublemakers were the only ones who let you." Clarice nodded. "I know. But you see, it's just a vicious circle, like a hamster on one of those wheels. They did this so you did that and then they did this. Around and around and around. The same territory. Never goes anywhere. Never makes any progress." She clapped Darcy on the shoulder.

"You're not a hamster, my dear. And it's time to get out of the rut."

"How?" It sounded wonderful; it would be great to get rid of this awful burden of guilt and anger. But Darcy had no idea how one accomplished that.

"Just step off," Clarice asserted. "Refuse to let yourself fall into the rut and dwell on the past again except to use it to figure out how to make the future better. Otherwise, you'll just get more and more bitter. And Jamie doesn't want a bitter mother."

"Jamie! Gosh, I forgot all about him for a moment." Darcy jumped up and hurried toward the door.

"He'll be fine. Luke knows how to handle children. Used to have one of his own."

The words stopped Darcy dead in her tracks. Now she'd find out more about the mysterious man who was always in the background, smoothing her way. She whirled around and peered at the older woman. "He's divorced?" she whispered.

"No." Clarice stared at her coffee cup, her face losing all of its angularity. "He's a widower. Lost his wife and daughter in a house fire three years ago. Your parents saved his life."

When it was clear that Clarice would say no more, Darcy crept from the room, her head whirling with what she'd just learned. The scars on his neck, she remembered. How did he get them? And what did Clarice mean that her parents had "saved" his life? Was that why he was here, living on this farm? Had Luke Lassiter become the son that Martha and Lester Simms had always wanted?

"Mommy, look!" Jamie's high-pitched voice penetrated her foggy brain, and Darcy glanced into the living room to find her son seated beside the ranch foreman; a huge book rested on their laps.

"Mister Luke is teaching me about cows and stuff." He beamed up at her, his little face shining with happiness. "This is a steer," he told her carefully, one chubby finger pointing to the photograph. "It's like the daddy. And this is a cow. She's the mommy."

"Yes, darling," she murmured. "But it's time for bed now. You'll have to talk more about ranching with Luke tomorrow." She held out her hand.

"But I can't go, Mommy. Mister Luke said he'd read me the story about all the animals going on a big boat." Jamie's earnest little face peered upward. "It's about when there was a flood," he whispered, eyes wide as saucers.

"Perhaps another time," Darcy murmured, helping him off the old worn sofa. "I'm sure Luke is busy with other things."

"Not too busy to read that," Luke murmured. "Would it be all right if I came up after he got into bed? I promise, I won't keep him up long."

He must miss the little nighttime rituals, Darcy

thought, staring into those warm brown eyes. She couldn't imagine how hard it must be for him. How hard it would be for her to go on if anything ever happened to Jamie! Surely she couldn't deny Luke this small comfort.

"All right," she agreed at last. "But just for ten minutes. It's already way past your bedtime."

"I know," Jamie agreed, walking along beside her and into his room. "And there's a lot of work to do on a ranch. You have to get up really, really early." He stood still while she tugged off his T-shirt and jeans, his blue eyes pensive. "I like it here," he declared at last.

"You don't mind staying in this room all by yourself?" With a pang of regret for the past, Darcy glanced around the space that had once been hers. The rock star posters were gone, of course. And the navy walls she'd insisted on had been painted over with a clean ivory. But there, against the closet, along the baseboards, she could still see the indentations of heel marks put there in frustration over a world that didn't give. There were too many memories, and Darcy concentrated on slipping on Jamie's pajamas.

"Nope, I like it in here." Jamie shook his tousled brown head firmly. "'Sides, Mister Luke is right over there." He pointed across the hall. "An' he promised he'd make sure no bad people came. I don't like bad people." A frown marred the smooth forehead. "I wish there was some kids, though. New York had lots of kids to play with. 'Cept Jeffrey Peterson. I hate Jeffrey Peterson!"

"Jamie," she scolded, "we don't 'hate' people."

"You do. I heard you on the airplane. You told

Mister Luke that you hated this place and everybody in it. I dunno why.'' He glanced around. ''I like it. It's nice and quiet. There's no bad men here, are there, Mommy? I don't like bad men.''

Trapped in the web of her own words, Darcy searched for an explanation. ''Listen, sweetie. I didn't really mean that I hated *everybody*. I was just upset.''

''Why?'' His blue eyes were quizzical. ''Mister Luke said this used to be your home. Didn't you want to come home no more?''

''Anymore. And no, honey. I didn't. I felt like nobody loved me or cared about me when I lived here, Jamie. I got into trouble, and people got mad at me and that made it worse.'' She took a deep breath. ''I felt like I was all alone.''

''But nobody's alone.'' Jamie patted her hand consolingly. ''Everybody has God watching them. God loves you, Mommy. Me, too!'' He threw his arms around her neck and hugged for all he was worth, and Darcy hugged him back, tears rolling down her cheeks.

''I love you too, darling. Very much.'' She let him pull away a bit and met his puzzled stare.

''Why are you crying? Do you have a hurt?'' He searched her face seriously. ''I could kiss it better, Mommy.''

''You already have,'' she whispered, hugging him close once more. ''You're the best medicine in the world.''

''An' I don't taste yucky, neither.'' Jamie grinned happily. ''Do I brush my teeth now, or after Mister Luke reads the story?''

''Oh, now I think.'' Darcy told herself to regain

some control. Her son wasn't going to have an emotional, out-of-control mother to look back on. "Come on, I'll watch. Be sure you do the back ones."

Ten minutes later Jamie was tucked up in bed, face shining, eyes huge with anticipation. "I'm ready, Mister Luke!" he called out. His smile grew when Luke stepped through the door.

"Are you sure it's all right?" Luke asked, glancing at Darcy for confirmation.

"*I'm* sure," Jamie answered for both of them. "Smell my hands." He held them up as Luke obediently bent over and sniffed the small fingers. "They smell like flowers. That's how you know I washed with soap and water. If you can't smell the flowers, you didn't wash," he quoted, grinning at Darcy. "Right, Mom?"

"Right, Love Bug. Into bed now."

Seconds later Luke launched into his story of Noah and the ark as Darcy listened from the hard-backed maple chair that matched her desk. She'd forgotten many of the details that Luke elaborated upon. Like a sponge, Jamie soaked in the old Bible story. Luke was a wonderful storyteller, and the boy's face glowed with amazement.

"Two of *everything?*" He frowned at Luke's nod. "But wouldn't the snakes eat the birds and the tigers gobble up the giraffes?" Jamie loved animals, and Darcy had read him thousands of books over the years. The little boy prided himself on knowing the eating habits of many of them.

"Well, you see, God had everything arranged, and I think He must have had a plan to prevent that. He wanted a mommy and a daddy of every kind of animal so that after they got out of the ark, they could have lots of babies together. Anyway, He kept His eye on them in that ark just like He does now, and helped Noah make sure that each one got enough to eat and drink.''

''Does God wear glasses?'' Jamie stared innocently up at Luke.

''I don't think He needs them,'' Luke answered thoughtfully. ''Why?'' There was a twinkle in his eye that Darcy didn't miss.

''You keep saying He kept his *eye* on them,'' Jamie explained patiently. ''I guess He must have pretty big eyes to see everything like that. I can't understand about eyes that big.''

''That's right, son. People can't understand God. Not even if they try very hard. The Bible says He's unfathomable. That's a big word that means we can't imagine what He is like.''

''Why?''

''Because we don't have anything to compare God with. God just is. He's big and great and powerful. He sees everything and knows everything.''

''Oh.'' Jamie appeared to be thinking that over, so Luke continued on with the story.

Darcy sat listening, her mind on those Sunday School sessions she had attended so long ago. She'd heard the stories a hundred times, knew some of them off by heart, and yet they'd never made as much sense as they did right now with Luke's explanation.

''But why did all the people do the wrong things?'' Jamie wanted to know.

''Everybody does wrong sometimes, son. There's no way we can help it because we're human. God made us and He knows that we're going to goof up." Darcy saw the tall man edge the quilt up a little higher on the bed, and smiled when Jamie wiggled out.

"But He doesn't care, right?"

"Oh, He cares all right, Jamie. Very much. And He understands. But He wants us to learn from our mistakes so we can get better at doing what He wants." Luke brushed the tousled curls back off the boy's face. "It's the same as if you took something from Aunt Clarice and then went and told her you were sorry. I'm sure she'd tell you she forgives you. But if you did the same thing tomorrow and then again the next day, I'm sure she would wonder if you were *really* sorry, or if you were just saying the words without meaning them."

"Uh-huh." Jamie's lids were drooping down, and Darcy rose from her chair.

"I think it's time you went to sleep, sunshine," she murmured, bending down to tuck him in once more. "Morning is going to come pretty early you know." She waited while Luke accepted another hug, and then took his place on the bed, snuggling her little boy in her arms. "Good night, Love Bug."

"She just calls me that—" Jamie yawned up at Luke "—I'm not really a bug. Good night, Mommy. I love you."

"I love you too, sweetheart. Very much. Sweet dreams," Darcy whispered, watching until the soft deep breaths of sleep told her that Jamie was resting in dream world. She clicked off the lamp and slipped out the door, checking first that his night-light was on.

"He's a wonderful little boy," Luke murmured as

he followed her down the stairs. "Full of love and so ready to give it out. I can't imagine how you've managed to do such a wonderful job raising him all by yourself and in such difficult circumstances."

"I had help at first," Darcy told him as she cleared up Jamie's blocks and toys from the living room floor. "I met an old lady named Mrs. Pearse on the train the day I arrived in New York. She needed someone to stay with her so she could continue to live in her house, and I guess I looked pretty healthy. We agreed that I would live in, do the housework and make the meals in return for board and room." Darcy sighed. "She was so kind about my pregnancy, even took me to see a doctor. After I had Jamie, she insisted he and I remain with her. She loved him like a grandmother, and he adored her. I was able to spend the first fifteen months of his life with him."

"What happened then?"

"She died, and I had to go to work. It seems ironic, but I got a job as a nanny. I had to send my own son out to someone else so I could look after this woman's children every day. I stayed there until I could get a job at a day care. That way Jamie was always nearby." Darcy stared out at the snow blowing across the yard and remembered those first years.

"God was certainly there with you, protecting you," Luke murmured.

"Was He?" Darcy laughed bitterly. "I wonder." She thought of the scrimping and saving she'd done, the desperate search for a place to stay when the Pearse family insisted that she move out. "I don't think He even noticed."

"Why do you doubt it, Darcy? He sent someone to watch over you. He gave you a healthy baby and time to bond with him before the world intruded. He was there, watching out especially for you, His child."

"And when the day care was taken over by people who insisted you needed certification to work there? Where was He then? Or when we got evicted, or when I had to move to keep from being attacked? How about that hole you found me in? Where was He when men stopped me on the street and harassed me and my son? Can you tell me that?" She yelled the words, furious at dredging it all up again.

"He was there, Darcy. All the time, He was there. You just had to call on Him."

"Don't you think I did?" Darcy felt the words explode from her as her fingers clenched into fists. "Don't you think I begged and pleaded for Him to help me find a way out? But it just got worse and worse until I was hanging on by a thread." She shuddered. "Do you know how many times I had to put Jamie to bed hungry because we didn't have anything and I was too afraid to leave my room at night?"

"I know it wasn't easy. And I admire you more than I can say for hanging on."

"Admire me?" She laughed bitterly. "Do you admire the fact that I've walked out of a place knowing I'd never be able to pay the rent I owe? Do you admire my stealing from someone's grocery bag so Jamie could have some milk?" She caught the sob in her throat and swallowed, refusing to give in to the tears.

"I came this close to giving him up for adoption,

you know." She shivered at the memory, her voice ragged. "This close." She held up thumb and forefinger, less than an inch apart.

"Why didn't you? It would have been much easier on you." Luke's voice was calm, as if he wasn't the least bit stunned by her revelations. "He might have had a wonderful life with some couple."

"And he might have been miserable, wondering why his mother had abandoned him. Wondering if I didn't love him anymore." Darcy shook her head vehemently. "I wasn't having my child grow up thinking I didn't care about him! Besides—" she made a face "—I'm not known for taking the easy route." Darcy sighed miserably. "I tried to tell myself that it would be the best thing for him if I gave him up for adoption. But I couldn't, I just couldn't walk away and let him go."

"Why not?" Luke stood just three feet away. His eyes were clear and focused on her, waiting for her answer.

Darcy laughed, a hard brittle sound that resounded in the room. "Because I loved him from the moment he was born. I loved watching him look at me with complete and utter faith that I would do the right thing. Jamie never imagined that his mother would leave him alone to face life—"

"Darcy, I didn't mean…"

She ignored his interruption, determined to make him understand that Darcy Simms was not who the good folk of Raven's Rest thought she was. "I couldn't do it," she whispered. "I just couldn't give him away, as if he was something I didn't want. He was the one good thing in my life, and I wasn't going to hand him over without at least trying to be his mother." She sniffed, remembering the wash of feelings as if it were yesterday.

"Jamie loves me. He gives that love freely just because I'm his mother. He doesn't care if I don't always do what everyone else expects. It doesn't matter to him if I bleached my hair in high school, or cheated on a math test, or broke Hettie Arbunson's picture window. He just loves me. How could I hand that over to someone else as if it didn't matter?"

There was silence in the room. Luke must be digesting her past misdeeds, and he must be shocked, Darcy decided sadly. The upright, law-abiding Simms family had failed to control her again. The reprobate daughter was impossible to repair. As the seconds ticked by, she shifted nervously from one foot to the other, gnawing at her bottom lip.

"Darcy?" Luke's voice was full of something. Was it—sympathy? No, not that. He was smiling as if she'd done something wonderful.

"Y-yes," she stammered, afraid to look any deeper into those chocolate-brown eyes. Afraid to believe what she saw there.

"How can you say that you got nothing but pain from life in Raven's Rest? You left with Jamie tucked under your heart. How much more could God have done than give you that precious gift? You wouldn't or couldn't understand His love, so He gave you the kind of love that you *could* understand."

"No." She shook her dark head adamantly. "I didn't love Jamie's father. I never deluded myself that our relationship was about love. Not after the first few minutes anyway. It was about me searching for someone who wanted me for myself, as a person, worthy of loving. And it was about a boy who saw me as an opportunity." Her lips tightened. "And then he dumped me like yesterday's news, just as his mother wanted."

"I'm not talking about that kind of love," Luke told her. "I'm talking about Jamie's kind of love. You made a mistake, trusted where you shouldn't have. We all do that. But out of that mistake came a wonderful little boy."

"That pregnancy was why I had to leave," she explained cooly. "It was the final straw, and my parents were disgusted by me."

"It doesn't matter what they thought, or what you thought they felt. God put you in charge of something so special. He entrusted Jamie to you. And then, far from abandoning you, He stayed right there to smooth the way." Luke shook his head in amazement. "A thousand terrible things could have happened to you and your son, Darcy. Unspeakable things. But you were kept safe, thank God. Secure in His tender care. Jamie told me he even had a personal baby-sitter that last week in New York."

Luke slowly ambled to the doorway, his eyes shining with a peculiar light as he tugged on his sheepskin jacket. His face was thoughtful as he crammed his Stetson onto his head. "I don't think that's the sign of a God who doesn't care about you, Darcy. I think that's the sign of a God who loves you more than you know."

The house was quiet when Darcy finally went to her room. Clarice had long since retired, and as the old house creaked and groaned in the wind, Darcy thought long and hard about what Luke had said. One by one, she recalled the coincidences that had kept her from becoming one of thousands of street kids who were barely surviving while trapped in the deepest of troubles in the middle of a city that neither knew nor cared about one girl's problems.

Maybe You were there, she conceded, staring at the ceiling. *Maybe You did care about me. But, oh, God, what is going to happen when I go to that school tomorrow and the rest of the town finds out that Darcy Simms, local bad girl, is just as rotten and lousy a daughter as she ever was?*

Chapter Six

"All right class, now let's listen to the next directions."

Darcy watched as the giggling group of kids obediently put down their crafts and watched their teacher. Clarice slowly demonstrated how to put a little slurry—the watery mixture of clay—on each coil before gently joining it to the next one. In the back row, a little girl sat struggling to fit the pieces together.

"Here, honey. You dip your finger like this into the jar and mix it against the clay a little." Darcy hunched down to show the child and found a big pair of gray eyes peering up at her.

"Thank you," the child murmured politely. "Sometimes my hands don't do what I want them to do. Or my feet."

Darcy tried not to glance down at the heavy braces on the child's legs. "What's your name?"

"Ginny. Ginny Jones."

Darcy took a second startled look and chided herself for not realizing it immediately. "Are you Jesse's
daughter?" she asked softly, aware of the sudden silence in the room. Clarice and Hilda Ridgely both
stared at her.

"Yes. Do you know my daddy?" The child's red
curls glowed in the late afternoon sun.

"I used to," Darcy told her. "We weren't in the
same grade, but he used to help me with my science
projects when I went to school here." She grinned
down at the little girl. "I'm afraid I was never very
good at science." Or a lot of other things, she almost
added.

"Mommy says Daddy is too smart for his own
good. And then Daddy says, 'René, you've got to
forget the past. I don't want to move away from
Raven's Rest with Dad so low.' Then they get all sad
and Dad goes outside." Ginny carefully pressed another ring onto her "sculpture."

It was an intimate look into someone's personal
life, and Darcy knew she had no business listening.
But she did, just the same, curiosity overwhelming
her good sense. René Carter had been voted the girl
most likely to succeed. Last Darcy recalled, René had
been intent on pursuing a scholarship that she'd won
at a prestigious fashion design school. Darcy could
well imagine that being stuck in this little town hadn't
been her first choice. Ginny's obvious physical difficulties would have made life here even more difficult.

A towheaded boy down the row claimed her attention then, and Darcy put the past firmly out of her
mind. By the time the bell rang, Clarice and Hilda
had managed to organize things so that all the stu-

dents' work was carefully stored under a big plastic sheet, ready for tomorrow's lesson.

"You have quite a rapport with children." Hilda peered over the tops of her bifocals to study Darcy with the same calculating look she'd used back when Darcy had misbehaved in her class all those years ago. "I don't suppose you've taken any training?" That disapproving look was back in her eyes. Nothing had changed in Miss Ridgely's class.

"No," Darcy admitted dryly. "I didn't have the money to go to school. Actually I never even thought of teaching. But I did enjoy today. Thank you for letting me help."

"My dear girl," Hilda puffed as she lifted a stack of books off a shelf. "In this place we never turn down an offer of help. And you have a natural gift with children. You always did."

Darcy stared at her. "I did?"

"Of course. That's why I asked you to help out the others so often. Surely you haven't forgotten Birdie McBride?"

Darcy searched her memory. "Birdie McBride? I don't think...wait a minute, you mean the little girl who wore those heavy leg things? She'd been in a car accident or something."

"It wasn't a car accident, it was polio. Her parents were missionaries and she contracted it as a baby, which meant she missed a lot of school." Miss Ridgely's dour face almost cracked in its smile. "You handled her better than I ever could have. I always feel pushed to get through the curriculum, and I just couldn't spare the time to go back over things that she should have learned before. But you sat with her, noon hour after noon hour, helping her to read."

The words were a balm on Darcy's aching heart. At least she'd done one thing right in her sojourn here. "But you never said anything," she muttered, frowning at her former teacher. "You never told me that."

"I wanted to. So many times I wanted to stop you and say 'Well done!'"

"Why didn't you?" Darcy asked bitterly. "It would have meant so much to know that I was doing something right in my mixed-up life."

"I tried to. I even called you up several times to suggest some colleges you might want to look into." Hilda shook her head sadly. "But you said you were too busy. Do you remember? I knew you were running with a bad crowd, and I was sure that if only you could get involved in planning the future, you'd forget those ne'er-do-wells and get back on the right track."

"I didn't know. I thought you wanted to bawl me out for something, just like everyone else." Dismay filled her at the missed opportunity. "I was so desperate for somebody to say something nice to me that I think I would have done anything to get some attention."

"But, Darcy," Hilda protested, laying a hand on her shoulder. "Your parents loved you very much. You must know that."

"Yeah, I should have known, shouldn't I?" Darcy refused to get maudlin about the past. She would deal with the here and now. "Anyway, thanks for the afternoon. I actually enjoyed it."

"There's a teacher's aide job that has been open for the past two months. No one seems to want to take it on." Hilda studied Darcy as if assessing her. "It's a good way to find out if that's the work for you. If you're interested, that is."

"But I don't know anything about teaching." Darcy stared at her. "I've never done anything like that before."

"And never will if you don't try it out," Clarice muttered, coming up behind them. "Get your application in to Hilda. She'll look after the rest."

Sheer panic swept over Darcy. She wasn't ready for this, her mind screamed. She didn't even want to stay in Raven's Rest.

"I...that is, I was hoping to spend more time with Jamie," she managed at last and then quelled a shudder as Hilda's hawklike glance moved over her. "He's my son," she said defensively.

"Job only involves two afternoons a week." Clarice offered the words quietly. "Jamie's lonesome. He might want to go to the preschool and play with other kids on those afternoons."

"Yes, I'll have a talk with the principal, get her to call you. She'll give you the specifics." Hilda grabbed her purse and a pen off the desk. "I have to run now. Staff meeting. Thanks so much, Clarice. And you too, Darcy. It's nice to see you again."

Darcy followed Clarice out of the school in total bemusement. Hilda hadn't said a word, not a word, about Jamie. Of course she was probably going to mention it in the staff room, telling everyone about the Simms girl. But at least Darcy didn't have to witness it.

Luke and Jamie were waiting outside the school in Luke's big truck.

"Hi!" Jamie leaned out the window, grinning from ear to ear. "We came to get some parts, and Mister Luke said we could stay and have coffee with you." He smiled at Clarice. "I never had coffee before."

"And you're not having any now, either." Darcy grinned as she kissed his cheek and ruffled his already messy hair. "I'm ready to go home."

"Have to get some things first—" Clarice chanted a list of destinations as she searched in her bag for her list "—the general store, the hardware store, the post office... You can go ahead if you like."

"Actually, I think we'd better stop at the grocery store." A picture of the almost-empty fridge flitted through Darcy's mind. "We need some milk, fresh fruit and vegetables for a salad."

"Okay, okay, ladies! But can't we stop for a coffee break first?" Luke's voice chided them plaintively. "I'm starved and cold. We were out mending fences all morning and my feet are numb."

"A bit parched myself," Clarice murmured. "Must be all that talking."

It was probably true, Darcy decided, watching the other woman run her tongue over her lips. She'd never heard Clarice say so much at one time since she'd met her.

They all trooped over to the café and Darcy found herself under Luke's steady gaze. "I'm buying," he told her firmly. "It's my treat."

There was nothing she could say but thank-you, since she had hardly any money. A job would come in really handy right now, she decided, thinking over

Hilda's words once more. At least she'd have pocket change.

"I forgot my gloves in the staff room." Darcy gave them a frustrated glance. "You guys go ahead and order. I'll catch up."

She hurried back to the school and rushed inside, heading for Hilda's room. But there were voices inside, and she stopped in her tracks at the familiar grumbling tones.

"I'm not having that *tramp* come into this school and work with impressionable children."

There was no mistaking the biting tones of her archenemy Annette Pickens.

"She's not a fallen woman," Hilda replied. "She made a mistake, and that was nearly *six years* ago! I daresay, we've all made a few of those—you included. And somebody managed to forgive us."

"Maybe. Still, she sails in here as if she's the queen of the castle, ready to show all us peasants how lucky we are to have us among her subjects. Well, I'm not giving her the job. Besides, she doesn't have any qualifications." Annette sounded triumphant over that, and Darcy almost laughed at the ridiculousness of it all. Surely after all these years, Annette wasn't still jealous?

"We need an aide, Annette. And Darcy Simms would make an excellent one. She's always done exceptionally well at teaching the younger children. Obviously that's carried over into her adult life. If you won't at least take her application and interview her, I'll speak to Roger about last Thursday."

"Hilda, that's blackmail! You can't tell him I went

out with Lenny Turbelo for dinner on Monday! He'll kill me!''

Darcy flushed at this personal knowledge of Annette's private affairs, wishing she'd never stopped, but unable to walk away.

"Maybe he will. Or maybe you two will have to sit down and make some compromises. It's ridiculous the way you keep battling each other for the upper hand in this relationship. Why don't you try working together by setting some common goals? That's the way a marriage is supposed to work.''

"As if you know anything about marriage," Annette replied. "You've never been married, so how would you know?''

"No, I haven't been married. But I've seen a lot of failed marriages, and I *do* know that the wrong thing to do when you're having problems is make your husband think you're two-timing him.''

There was the scraping of a chair, and Darcy held her breath as she backed carefully away from the door. Then she turned, racing down the hall and back out the door she'd entered only moments ago.

Of all the hateful people to run into, Annette was just about the absolute worst. She'd hated the fact that Josiah and Darcy had grown so close in high school, and she'd never forgiven Darcy for taking him away from her. And now she was going to try to prevent Darcy from taking this job as an aide?

"Over my dead body, Annette.'' She muttered the words to herself, stomping through the snow to the café. "I *want* that job, I *deserve* that job—and I'm going to *have* that job.''

* * *

"You look mad about something." Luke raised one curious eyebrow as he relieved her of her jacket and ordered another coffee. "Did something happen? I see you didn't find your gloves."

"No, I didn't. I guess I'll just have to go back. Maybe I can do it when I go in to fill out the job application." She explained the aide position to him.

"Sounds like a good opportunity." He grinned. "Go for it."

"I just might. Hey, maybe we can see the lawyer while we're here," she murmured, accepting the coffee mug and a thick piece of blueberry pie. "I'd like to start getting things sorted out."

"I don't think he's back yet, but we'll stop and find out." Darcy didn't miss the glance that Luke shot across to Clarice.

"Is there something I should know?" she asked quietly. "Something about the ranch? Is it in trouble?"

"No, it's not in trouble." Luke sipped slowly from his steaming cup. "These last few years, the ranch has done very well."

Darcy bit into her pie with gusto, relieved to hear that she wouldn't be any further in debt. "Then there shouldn't be any trouble with the will," she mumbled, relishing the sweet fruity filling that had never tasted so good anywhere else. But then she saw a strange look pass over Luke's face. "Should there?" she asked cautiously.

"Not trouble exactly. Darcy, there's something I've been meaning to say—"

He stopped when a tiny round woman toddled up beside them. "Hello, Mrs. Lancaster. Chilly day, isn't it?'' He waited a moment for her response and lost total control of the conversation.

"My word, Clarice, don't you look spiffy! I haven't seen you in anything but pants for so long, I wasn't sure you owned any skirts.'' Her narrowed eyes slid over Clarice and settled on Darcy. "Finally made it back, did you? And a bit late at that. Where were you anyway, that you couldn't come home to see your parents when—''

"I'm sure Darcy appreciates your condolences, Mrs. Lancaster.'' Luke interrupted the conversation in a loud voice. "But I think she's just a bit overwhelmed with everything since she arrived. Things have changed quite a bit in five years.''

Darcy glared up at the one person in Raven's Rest who could distort fact faster than any other. "This is my son, Mrs. Lancaster. His name is Jamie. He'll be five years old in January.'' She laid out the facts deliberately, waiting for those black eyes to count backward and figure it all out.

"Your son? But your parents didn't say anything about a child.'' Mrs. Lancaster peered down at Jamie, who sat placidly tolerating the scrutiny.

"They didn't know. And yes, I have been raising him on my own in New York from the day he was born. We managed just fine, thank you. But now we're back. For a while.'' She dared the woman to ask anything more.

"He does resemble your mother, rest her soul.'' The woman's eyes shifted to meet Darcy's glare head-on. "And I suppose you've come home to find a father for the boy. Sensible, my dear. Very sensible. And Luke is perfect, what with him being half owner of the ranch and all.'' Ella Lancaster gathered up her bags of groceries.

"I must say, however, that there will be a few broken hearts left around here. Jalise Penner won't be at all happy that yet another man's been taken off the market. She had her cap set on Luke there, and she won't take kindly to rearranging it at this late date. Ta ta.'' And with that bombshell, she scurried away.

"Of all the rude, overbearing people,'' Darcy seethed. "I can understand how her husband needs to disappear into the mountains, alone, for weeks at a time. It's a wonder he doesn't stay there permanently.'' She glanced round the table, her eyes settling on Luke's whitened face.

"What a pile of hogwash. As if my parents would leave half the ranch to you—'' the shocked look on Clarice's face stopped her from continuing "—what's the matter?''

"Darcy, you need to hear something before this gets any further.'' Clarice's tones were soft but firm, and the hand she laid on Darcy's was compelling. "Promise me that you'll listen to Luke. Please?''

Darcy stared at first one, then the other. Enlightenment dawned slowly. "Then it's true?'' she gasped as an arrow of sheer pain stabbed straight into her heart. "My own parents chose someone else over me to leave their worldly goods to?'' The shadows chasing over Luke's brown eyes told her the truth.

"They didn't know where you were, Darcy,'' Luke told her. "And they were afraid that if they didn't set something up, if someone wasn't in control, the ranch would get eaten up by the banks or be left to run down. They didn't want that to happen.''

"No, what they didn't *want* was Disappointing Darcy to get one thin dime of theirs without paying the tune! Tell me," she demanded bitterly, "do I have to live here for a year or two before I have legal claim to my half?" At the expression on his pale face, Darcy laughed, her voice full of unshed tears. "I thought so."

"Not a year," Luke murmured. "Six months. I'm sorry. I was trying to tell you."

"Of course you were! Sooner or later, right?" She studied her son, who was happily playing with his little car. "Tell me, Luke—what happens if I walk out that door and never return to Raven's Rest?"

His eyes widened, but he answered in the same calm tones. "You lose your right to half."

"Just like that. As if I'd never even been here." Darcy snapped her fingers. "Isn't that something? Even in death, five years after the fact, they're still trying to manipulate me."

"It isn't like that," he protested softly. "They just wanted you to come home one last time. To see that things had changed, that they had changed. It is only for six months. After that, you're free to leave if you want to. And I'll buy you out."

"Yes, with my other half of the inheritance!"

Darcy rolled the whole messy situation around in her mind. Free to leave? That was a joke! She didn't have enough money for the bus fare to Denver, let alone enough to rent a place and start over again. No job, no prospects. And a child to look after. Leaving Raven's Rest now wouldn't be the simple affair that it had been the first time around.

Fine. If they had wanted her back here, her parents

had finally gotten their wish. She was here. She was staying, for a while at least. And she intended to find out everything she needed to know about how to get what was rightfully, *by birth,* her legacy.

"I want to see everything," she told him fiercely. "I want to see the books, the bank statements—everything." He nodded curtly. "Have you been drawing a salary since they died?"

"Yes, the same as when they were alive. Nothing has changed."

Darcy ignored that. For her, *everything* had changed. Forget about love, forget about trying to make amends. There wasn't any point now. It didn't matter. What did matter was getting some security out of this fiasco for herself and her son. She didn't begrudge Luke any of what her parents had left. He could have it with her blessing. But she would take her fair share, too. After all, they owed her that much. Didn't they?

"And Clarice?" She hated saying it, hated the ugly, greedy way it came out. But she had to know exactly where she stood and how many other surprises there were waiting in the wings.

"I'm just staying for Luke's sake," the other woman replied. "I helped your mother out, but since she died, I've been keeping up the house and providing meals as best I could." Her thin angular face was intent. "I don't want any money, Darcy. I have my pension. But I would like to help out on the ranch if I can. Maybe I could watch Jamie for you once in a while."

Darcy nodded, but her mind was busy sorting it all out. "I want you to set up a bank account for me," she informed Luke in a cold hard voice. "And I want the same salary as you." She held up a hand to forestall his protests. "I'm perfectly willing to work for it, but I need some money to support Jamie and myself until this will thing is settled."

"I don't have any objections." He nodded, his eyes soft and compassionate. "It's not that much, actually." He told her the amount and shrugged at the skepticism on her face. "Your dad and I had a deal. He helped me learn ranching, and I helped him with the physical stuff. I got my room and board free and a couple of head for my own at the end of the year, if we made a profit."

"Fine." The sum Luke had mentioned wouldn't go very far in New York, Darcy knew. If she wanted to get out of this place and back on her own, she'd need to supplement it somehow. Hilda Ridgely's words rumbled across her brain. The teacher's aide position might help. And it would look good on a resume.

"If you would rather Clarice move to her own place…" Luke began, his mouth pursed into a narrow disapproving line.

"No, not at all. I'd appreciate it if she could stay and watch Jamie for me two afternoons a week. And maybe an evening or two—I'm not sure about that right now." If Hilda knew what she was talking about, Darcy should be able to find out how to start the courses necessary to teach. She would not leave this town defenseless and ill-equipped to earn her living. *Not again.*

"Darcy, we had no intention of deceiving you." Luke leaned across the table, his hand touching hers until she yanked it away. "We just didn't know how to tell you."

"I can imagine." She held his steady gaze, daring him to look away.

"It's true, honey. Lucas didn't want any part of it, but then when we couldn't find you and things needed handling...well, someone had to step in." Clarice stood from the table. "I don't want to put upon anyone. I'll pack my things and be out by tomorrow morning." She left so quickly, in those jerky sparrow-like movements, that Darcy didn't have time to stop her.

"You've hurt her feelings." Luke's warm gaze had cooled somewhat. "You didn't have to do that."

"I never meant to! I just don't want any more secrets." Darcy swallowed the angry thoughts of her parents' deceit and concentrated on the glossy tabletop. "I can deal with hard reality, you know. It's not knowing what's coming next that gets to me."

"I never set out to get half of your ranch, Darcy. But when your father asked me if I'd run things and watch out for you, I agreed because I knew he needed the help and it would take a worry off his mind." His face tightened. "He had enough pain, Darcy. Agreeing to take over the ranch and run things with you was the least I could do."

"Pain? What pain?" Darcy frowned. "You keep acting as if he was sickly or something. My father was always as healthy as a horse."

"Are you certain you want to hear the truth, Darcy? All of it? Because I guarantee that it isn't pretty." He waited for her nod before drawing in a deep breath. "Your father had liver cancer. A lot of the time he was in agony, and the painkillers couldn't seem to touch it.''

"Liver cancer? Oh, no! I never knew—didn't even guess." She felt the color drain from her face and clutched the edge of the table for support. Then she rushed blindly for the door. Outside, in the cold brisk air, she headed for the park, drawing in deep cleansing breaths. *Cancer?* Her father?

"Are you all right?"

She was startled to see Luke standing beside her, Jamie at his side—both of them out of breath from trying to catch up to her. For a moment, she'd even forgotten about Jamie!

"Yes." She walked down the pathway between the overhanging boughs of pines that sheltered them from the wind. "Thanks," she added belatedly.

Jamie spied the playground equipment and raced off to climb on it. When he was safely out of earshot, Darcy turned to Luke.

"Okay, tell me all of it."

"It was a real blessing from God that he died when he did, Darcy. He was on his way to another chemo treatment. They were going to stay in Denver overnight and come home the next day. Your mother insisted on going along to keep him company, even though she couldn't possibly have handled the car. Clarice went to drive him back."

"Why couldn't my mother drive?" Darcy felt a frisson of fear. "Why?" she demanded when he didn't speak.

"She was too crippled by arthritis then, Darcy. I think she went along just to spend more time with him. Your father said riding in the car with your mother was more soothing than all the pain pills the doctors could prescribe. Your mother had her own medication for pain by then.''

"She was bad, then?" Darcy whispered the words, not wanting to hear it confirmed, yet somehow needing to.

His arm curved round her shoulders, hugging her close for support. "She'd had several operations to try and straighten her joints, but nothing seemed to take." He handed her a tissue and took another deep breath. "Clarice came because I asked her to. I interviewed some home-care people, but no one wanted to stay when they found out how far we were from the city. I was desperate for someone to help. Clarice sold her house on a moment's notice and came without asking any questions. She and your mother bonded the moment they met."

Darcy gulped down the sobs that rose in her throat. She'd been so thoughtless to the one person who had made her mother's last days tolerable. How could she look Clarice in the eye again?

"How did they die?" It hurt to ask, and Darcy clenched her fists to maintain her control.

"Your dad always felt good for a few hours after the treatment. Relatively good, that is. Then the nausea kicked in. Lester said that while he was feeling good, he wanted to look at the fall colors. Your mother insisted on going along. They begged Clarice to relax, leave them alone together for a bit." Luke kicked one booted toe against the grass. "He said he was well enough to drive."

Darcy could hear the regret tinging his voice, and

knew then how much he had truly cared for her parents. "And?"

"A semi was coming from the opposite direction. Apparently its brakes failed and the driver couldn't stop. Your dad didn't have a chance to get out of the way." He glanced at her. "I'm sorry."

"It's all right," she murmured, clenching her jaw. "I had to know. I suppose it was better to hear it from you."

"Maybe. Anyway, that's what happened." His look told her that he didn't quite know what she would do with the information. "They're buried in the graveyard by the church," he said. "Harvey Withers told me they'd chosen the lots a long time ago."

"I figured as much." Darcy smiled grimly. "They always did put the church first."

"Not the church, Darcy. *God.* That's the way it should be, don't you think?"

But Darcy didn't know what she thought anymore. She only knew that her parents were gone and she felt alone. More alone than she had in years. And now the ranch—the one thing of theirs that they could have trusted her with—didn't belong to her. Not really.

"I have to go over to the feed store. Is it okay if Jamie comes with me?" Luke's eyes met hers with a sympathetic look. "You could go on over to the church, if you wanted," he suggested diffidently. "I'll be ready to leave in about an hour."

It was better than sitting in his truck, having the entire population staring at her, Darcy decided. She stood watching Jamie as he slid down the curly slide, his face glowing from the cold. Nobody could make her feel guilty about him, though. Jamie wasn't a mistake. Her child was the one good thing in her life.

"All right." She agreed finally, ignoring the reservations she felt. She would have to go to the cemetery sooner or later.

"I'll meet you back here at five." She headed toward the far side of the park. But something stopped her. Turning, she cast Luke a glance. He was standing where she'd left him, his dark eyes following her. "Thanks," she murmured.

He nodded. "You're welcome." His big wide smile made her feel strangely comforted, and Darcy set off again, determined to at least look at the new graves.

As she went, her mind replayed his words. *They put God first. Isn't that the way it should be?*

Maybe, a nasty little voice inside chided her. But they should have put you second. Instead you came in dead last.

That was enough to send her racing across the grass, forcing herself to move so fast that her lungs begged for relief. At least it stopped the tears from coming.

When she got to the church, there were people in the adjoining graveyard. Darcy had no intention of wandering around looking like a fool as she hunted for her parents' graves, so she walked inside the church to wait. Someone was practicing on the organ and the light melodic notes carried through the building, hanging suspended from the cathedral ceiling as they resounded around the sanctuary.

It was a familiar room. She'd been here hundreds

of times, often not of her own will but out of a sense of duty. Her parents had always sat in the pew at the front. And over there was the pew she'd shared with her friends a long time ago. Darcy knew that if she kneeled and looked under the bench, she'd find her initials carved into the seat. She could still feel the sting of punishment for that misdeed.

And there, by the altar, was where she'd prayed long and hard. With her whole heart, she'd begged God to change her, to make her into the kind of person someone could love. Too bad He hadn't answered. At least not in the way she meant. The one intimate experience Darcy had shared with another human being couldn't possibly be called love.

"Hello! I didn't hear you come in."

Darcy whirled around to find a tall, slim man behind her. He wore faded denims and a tattered cotton T-shirt, and his hair looked as if he'd been raking his fingers through it for hours.

"I don't usually practice when anyone is around. My mom says I need to ease up on the loud pedal. Anyway, most of the people in this congregation don't like my kind of music." He grinned, his face wreathed in boyish charm.

"That wasn't church music," she pointed out carefully. "It was too fast."

"I know." He grinned again. "I do it that way on purpose, just to keep up my fingers. If I only played the way they sang, my hands would have rigor mortis by the end of the first verse." He thrust out his tanned arm. "Kenny Anderson."

"Darcy. Darcy Simms." She shook his hand

quickly and then pulled back when the look of sympathy flooded his face.

"I'm sorry about your parents." His voice hinted at her loss without becoming maudlin. "They were really nice people. Our youth group went out there lots of times. They sure did like kids."

All except their own, Darcy felt like telling him. But she only smiled and nodded. "Thanks. Do you know where they're buried? I thought I'd take a look."

"Yeah, sure." He sent her a funny look that Darcy couldn't interpret. "We were all here, you know. The youth group, I mean. My dad let us take part in the funeral."

"Your father did?" Darcy wondered why the man had organized her parents' funeral.

"David Anderson. He's the pastor here." Kenny watched her for a moment before leading the way outside. "We've been here for about two years. The Pringles were gone long before we got here." It was a nonchalant comment meant to convey a friendly bit of information, but it sent a clench of fear to her stomach.

"W-where did they go?" Darcy asked, moistening her lips.

"I forget." The boy, Kenny, wrinkled his forehead. "Someplace west, I think. Did you know that the oldest boy and girl were married before they left?" When Darcy didn't say anything, he nodded. "Yes. Joe married some girl from Denver. I think they're missionaries in Brazil now. And Brenda met some guy at Bible School. They're pastoring down south."

"Oh." It was the most she could get out.

"Here they are. Right beside each other. They liked to be together, didn't they?" Kenny smiled at the two mounds placed side by side on the hillside. "We came with fresh flowers every day before it got so cold."

"That was nice," Darcy murmured, unable to stop staring at the two graves. She was alone, all alone in the world.

The wind whipped down the hill and tugged at her hair, tossing it wildly. Stabbing cold hit her full in the face, stinging her eyes. Kenny murmured something and walked away. But still Darcy couldn't leave. She stared at the final resting place of her parents as bitter tears coursed down her cheeks.

"If I had known you were ill, I would have come back," she whispered, sinking to her knees. "I don't know what we could have said that hadn't already been said over and over, but I wish I'd known."

The wind was howling now, tearing through the almost bare trees and driving the dry, crunchy leaves into a whirling frenzy. The sun shone, its watery yellow doing nothing to dispel the chill that held her there, unmoving on the hard ground.

"I have a son, you know. Your grandson. His name is Jamie. He looks like you, Mom." From somewhere on the other side of the hill, there were voices, but they quickly died away. "He's a wonderful little boy and I will never regret that I kept him. He loves me." She said the words boldly.

"Jamie doesn't care about people's rules. He doesn't know that I'm bad. He just loves me because I'm Mommy. The same as I loved you."

It hurt to say the words that had been jammed inside for so long. Her throat clogged with emotion. There was no answer from them. There couldn't be. They had gone to a place that she couldn't reach, and never would. And they'd gone together, leaving her behind. *Alone.* Alone with the memories of their bitter recriminations.

Do you think you can just stay here? Act as if there's nothing wrong with a single girl having a baby? How can you do that to us? Do you think everyone will just forget your transgressions? Remember, there is a cost for every crime. You've chosen to have a child without a father. You'll have to explain that to him someday. You can tell him why his mother wouldn't give him the chance at life in a happy family where two parents would provide for him. We won't be part of your deceit, Darcy. It's time to face your sins.

The feeling overwhelmed her like a black cloud of smoke. Every word inside begged for release and yet the ache was so great. But there was so much that needed to be said. She *needed* to say it, to let go of the bitterness that had festered inside for five long years.

"Why didn't you love me, Mom and Dad? What did I do that was so terrible? Didn't you want children?" The thought suddenly occurred to her, but was just as quickly tossed away. They'd loved having the youth group, Kenny had said. Clarice—or maybe it was Luke—had said much the same thing. So it was just her. There was something wrong with her.

"I've felt it for as long as I can remember," she said quickly, tracing a tiny cross in the dirt with one finger. "It wasn't that you didn't try. You provided for my physical needs very well, better than I've done for Jamie sometimes. But I didn't belong in your heart, and I knew it. The two of you made a circle and I couldn't get in no matter how hard I tried.'' She pushed the hair out of her eyes.

"I know you were disappointed in me. I disappointed myself long before I got pregnant. But Jamie is a wonderful little boy and I could never have given him away. He's a part of me.

"All I ever wanted was love. I wanted to know that no matter what happened, you would always love me just because I was your child. Was that so wrong?"

Still, the two graves lay silent.

"Darcy?" The word was almost whispered. She could hear it even though the wind had gained force, pulling and tugging at the down-filled jacket she'd left undone. She glanced up, noticing the tiny snowflakes dancing in the air.

Luke stood behind her, his sheepskin jacket tugged up around his ears and his hands protected from the weather by thick leather gloves. There were twinkles of light coming from behind his head, and Darcy stared, mesmerized by their colors.

"It's pretty," she murmured. "Like a kaleidoscope. Can I see?" She reached out to touch the glittering lights, striving to warm herself in their heat before the world went black.

Luke grabbed her as she swooned, and swung her up in his arms. She weighed next to nothing, he noted absently, striding across the grounds to where the truck sat purring by the church. He set her carefully inside, one hand brushing over the pale thin cheek.

"Lord, she's frozen!" he whispered as he did up her seat belt and slammed the door closed.

Luke raced around the truck and clambered in, flicking the heater up another notch in the already warm cab. In one swift movement, he'd shed his jacket and wrapped it around her.

There was nothing else in the cab to cover her with. Nor was there anything in the back. He was just going to have to head for home, Luke decided grimly. He hoped the storm that he could see brewing in the west would hold off until they got there. At least Clarice and the boy would be safe on the farm by now. He offered a word of thanks heavenward that he'd found his aunt outside the drugstore and sent the boy home with her.

Darcy moaned a little and shivered, hunching herself into her jacket. "C-c-cold," Darcy whimpered.

He didn't think she was awake. Just in case, he slipped his hand over hers and squeezed.

"I'm here, Darcy. I'm taking you home. We'll get you warm pretty soon."

She didn't respond, so he concentrated on his driving for a few minutes, then he tried again.

"Darcy," he called gently. "Darcy, can you wake up now?" He eased around an even bigger pile of snow and made the last turn toward home. "Darcy?"

He maneuvered his way through the gates, giving thanks as he drove up to the porch with a song of praise on his lips. *Thank you, Father.*

Luke jumped out of the truck, not caring that the cold ripped through his thin woolen shirt. He stalked around the powerful engine, through the drifts, and pulled open her door, gathering Darcy's lax body into his arms.

"Come on," he murmured tenderly, easing her out. "We're home now. You can have a nice hot bath."

"Home?" She opened one eye and peered up at him. "I'm cold, Luke, and my throat hurts. A lot. Could you get me some blankets?"

"Sure I will. Soon as we get inside. Just stay put now." She snuggled against him, and he sighed in relief, heading for the front door that swung wide open at their arrival. "Thanks, Clarice."

"It's me!" Jamie peered out from behind the door, smiling proudly. "Why are you carrying my mom?"

"Just close the door now, will you? That's a good boy. Where's Auntie Clarice?" Luke searched the living room as he deposited Darcy on the sofa.

"I'm looking after her. She's sick." He stopped talking and smiled as a faint voice hailed him from down the hall. "I gotta go," he said gravely. "Aunt Clarice wants a drink."

"Could I take it to her while you stay here and make sure your mommy doesn't fall off the couch? She's not feeling very well either, and you and I will have to get her to bed after I tell Clarice I'm home. Okay?" he asked quickly, as Clarice's voice called out again, more frantic now.

"I guess so." Jamie nodded in agreement as he perched himself on the floor beside his mother's feet.

Luke raced down the hall to find Clarice, white-faced and shaking, trying to lever herself out of bed. "You're sick, Clarice. Get back into bed."

"Never get sick," the woman denied angrily.

"Tough old bird like me doesn't cave in like that. My back's out is all. Medication makes me so tired. I was afraid Jamie was in trouble."

"He's fine. But if you don't cave in and lie down, you're going to fall down." Luke grinned. "Now, get in to bed or I'll have to report you to Jamie."

"Just for a minute," she finally agreed, flopping back on the pillows with obvious relief. "Till I get my sea legs again. Or my back straightens out." She was exhausted, and Luke knew she'd be snoring before he left the room. He headed back to the living room.

"Mommy?" Jamie whispered, watching as Darcy tried to stand.

"Darcy, it's Luke. Easy, honey. Just sit down. That's a girl." He grabbed her hand from behind and held on tightly in case she fought against him. He needn't have worried. Darcy sagged against him as if her stuffing had been removed. He kept his voice low and soothing, knowing Jamie was watching everything.

"Sit down, Darcy. You're sick and you need to rest." He sat down beside her, curving one arm around her shoulders when she laid her head on his chest.

"I'm not so bad, Luke. Am I? Doesn't God care about me at all?" The sad, defeated words stabbed him to the heart with their plaintive request for reassurance.

"Of course God cares about you! God loves you. He always has. You just wouldn't let Him for a while." He brushed the silken strands off her forehead and pressed his lips there, cradling her tenderly in his arms.

"I wouldn't?"

"No. But He didn't go away. He's still here, loving you. Because He's your heavenly Father and you are more precious to Him than anything else in the world." Jamie was staring at them, and Luke patted the seat beside him, inviting the boy closer.

Darcy shook her head. "God's mad at me."

"Oh, Darcy!" He felt his heart wrench. How had it happened that this beautiful woman felt so unloved? "God isn't mad at you. He knows you've been through some really tough times, and He's been there all along, waiting for you to ask Him for help."

She sighed miserably. "I've just goofed up one too many times. I wish it was true, though." Her eyes were wide and unfocused. "I'd like someone to love me."

"There is no limit to God's love. And I know He wouldn't refuse to forgive you, if you asked. He loves you, Darcy."

"No." She straightened, shaking her head vehemently. "Three times you're out." Her voice was higher now, and Luke could hear the frenzy building. "I struck out way more than that."

"Listen to me, Darcy. This is a verse from the Bible. It tells us about what God is really like." Luke heard the words whispered in his head even as he recited them: "'The Lord your God is a merciful God; He will not abandon you or destroy you.'" He cleared his throat. "It's a promise, Darcy. And God doesn't go back on His promises."

"Are you sure?" Her scared voice broke the long silence that dragged between them.

"I'm positive. 'He who is the Glory of Israel does not lie or change his mind; for He is not a man, that He should change His mind.' You see, when God says something, He means it."

"But you don't know what I've done—the things I've said. Nobody could forgive all that." She coughed, trying to clear her raspy throat.

"No, a person couldn't," he agreed, threading one hand through Jamie's soft fall of hair. "But this is God and He is very clear about loving us just the way we are. He doesn't leave any room for maybes."

"I can't think," she told him. "I feel funny. And my throat hurts again." Her blue eyes lit up as they focused on her son. "Hello, sweetheart. Did you have fun with Clarice?"

But Jamie merely stared at her, his frown wrinkling the smooth skin of his forehead.

She tried to stand in order to move toward him, but she wavered and grabbed Luke's arm.

"Oh, my. The whole room is spinning. Jamie, did you see those stars?"

She sagged against Luke, and he caught her close, his fingers slipping to her forehead. She was warm and he guessed she'd developed a fever.

"I'm cold," she muttered, snuggling against him. "Why is it so cold? I just have a little sore throat. Nothing to get silly about."

Luke wondered privately just how long she'd been nursing that "little" sore throat. Probably for weeks, if he was any judge of things.

"I don't see any stars. Where are the stars, Mister Luke?"

"Jamie, we need to get your mom to her room. She's sick." He scooped the slight form into his arms and started for her bedroom.

"My mom doesn't never get sick," Jamie proclaimed, trailing along behind. "Not never."

"Now where have I heard that before, Lord?" Luke grinned wryly as he set her on the bed.

"Jamie, could you get my nightgown?" Darcy asked. "It's in the bathroom. L-luke, you can leave now," she chattered, shivering.

Luke left the room and flicked up the thermostat in the living room. After a few minutes he went back into Darcy's room, where she was huddled under the covers, shivering even harder than before. "Why can't I get warm?"

"Because you sat outside, on the ground, in the middle of a Colorado blizzard, with nothing to protect you from that icy wind," he pointed out. "How long were you there?"

"I don't know. It doesn't matter." She closed her eyes and snuggled under the blankets. "I'll be fine in the morning."

"I'll go get some aspirin and hot water bottles. Jamie, want to help?"

"I want to stay with my mom." The child had perched himself on the side of the bed and was staring at Darcy with a worried frown. Luke knew her condition had affected him, but right now there was nothing he could do to reassure Jamie. Watching his mother for a few moments might help. Once she fell asleep, though, Luke would try to comfort the child.

But a few minutes later, as he tucked the warm bottles against her icy toes, Luke couldn't help wondering who would comfort the woman who lay dozing on the bed.

All I ever wanted was love, she'd said in that hurt little-girl voice out there by her parents' graves.

Luke couldn't help thinking that the needy child inside was still searching for the thing she had missed out on so long ago. And he had no idea how anyone would penetrate those barriers she kept so firmly in place. How could he help her find what she needed?

Only You, Lord, he prayed in his mind, sinking into the hard-backed chair that sat near the window. *Only You know the way out of this.*

Chapter Seven

"I have a lot to do," Darcy croaked, her throat on fire. "I can't afford to lie around like this."

"You're not going anywhere." Luke glared down at her.

"And I suppose you're going to stop me?" Darcy would have liked to scream her frustration, but the pain that would cause wasn't worth thinking about. "Look, I'm a partner in this place. I need to do my share." She coughed a little, trying to catch her breath as the pain seared her chest.

"You will. But not today." His tone was matter-of-fact. As if someone had appointed him her guardian, she fumed inwardly.

"Darcy, you've been fighting this thing for three days and just missed getting pneumonia. Yesterday a thaw set in outside, but this is the first morning you've been lucid for more than thirty minutes. The doctor said bed rest—and that's what you're having."

"I have to look after my son. Where is he?" She

glanced around the room, trying to see past the tall bossy man standing in her doorway.

"He's eating breakfast. Then he's coming with me. I've got some cattle stuck up on the north ridge and I have to go round them up. Jamie will be fine. My concern is you."

"You're not taking him on some expedition into the hills?" She choked it out, incensed by the very idea of her small defenseless son out in the frigid winter weather. "He's just a little boy!"

"He's a smart little boy who wants to learn more about ranching. And I'm going to teach him while you lie in that bed and regain your strength."

"There's nothing wrong with my strength," she burst out, unable to control her temper one moment longer. "I'm fine."

Darcy flipped the bedclothes back and swung her pajama-clad legs over the side, wincing at the aches and pains her body was rapidly relaying to her brain. She grabbed the night table and stood...for about thirty seconds, until the room began to whirl around crazily and she sat back down.

Tears formed on her lashes and dropped down her cheeks. Why did nothing in her life ever go right? She'd intended to apply for that job at the school and now she couldn't even stand, let alone deal with thirty rambunctious kids.

"The doctor said your reserves have been drained, Darcy. He thinks you've been running on nerves for far too long. So do I. You need to focus on recharging those batteries you've run down. And then you can worry about looking into schools." Luke's voice was more gentle than she'd ever heard it and Darcy couldn't help staring at him.

"How did you know about my plans to study?" she demanded in her squawky voice.

"You've been mumbling about them for the past three days," he said, smiling. "Between that and ranting about some broken vase, you had quite a time. Personally, I think it's a great idea to plan for the future. But you can't do anything until you get yourself strong. And that's going to take time."

Darcy peered up at him. There was admiration in his tone, as if he approved of her plans. Not that it mattered, she reminded herself.

"You don't think it would take too much time away from the ranch? After all, I want to pull my weight." She frowned. "I can't take the wages if I don't do the job."

With a start, she realized that she had just admitted she fully intended to hang around for a while.

"Darcy, I don't need help with the animals or the fences. I've got a hired man for that. But it would be nice to have hot meals at night and clean clothes for the morning. Not that I'm asking you to be a maid or anything!"

Darcy rolled her eyes. "Good." She chuckled. "I'm not a very good maid. But that's hardly doing enough when you're outside working all day. There must be something else."

He bit his lip, wondering whether or not to suggest it. It would give her a clearer picture of what he was trying to do with the ranch, and he wouldn't mind passing it over to her.

"I could show you how to keep the books," he

said at last, watching for some sign that she hated the idea. "It takes me far too long to balance the statements, and the ledger is way out of date."

Far from being dismayed, Darcy seemed pleased that he would ask. "Books I can do," she said. "I'll get you to show me how you've been handling things and take over right away. Then I'll keep them up after Jamie's in bed or when my other work is done."

"All right, I get the picture!" He held up his hand, laughing at her sincerity. "But you can't do it all right now. You're as weak as water. Yesterday you could barely sit up in bed for more than twenty minutes. You're not quite ready to take on the world today."

"You mean you've been looking after me?" The thought brought a flush of embarrassment to her cheeks. "Why? Where's Clarice?" She needed to see the older woman, to apologize for her unkind remarks. "She's not gone, is she?"

He shook his dark head. "No." His eyes glinted in the morning sun that flooded the room. "She's flat on her back in her room. Clarice pulled something she shouldn't have on the day of the storm and she's had to stay put."

"Oh, I'm sorry," Darcy murmured, genuinely distressed at the thought of that strong wiry woman having to stay still. "What happened?"

"What happened is that she's as stubborn as you! She insisted on lugging in a great big box of clay that she'd picked up earlier. Apparently she got it into the house all right, but going down the stairs, she missed a step and wrenched her back."

"Why didn't she just leave it till the blizzard was over?"

"Good question. I asked her that yesterday." His tone was unrepentant. "Apparently raw clay cannot freeze or it's no longer any good for throwing or firing. When she got home, the thermometer was in the low thirties, so she didn't want to leave it out in the car. It costs quite a bit to get the stuff shipped up here because it weighs so much. No way was she going to waste it." He snorted indignantly. "As if it was worth all the trouble it's caused. I'm so tired of people doing stupid things to save a dollar."

"Maybe that's because you have so many dollars. Or maybe it's because you've never had to watch them leave faster than they arrived." Her voice cracked and almost gave way. "When you get a dime, you learn to stretch it out and make every penny count. Believe me, I know."

"Frugality is fine. But I can afford to buy my aunt another box of that stuff if she needs it."

"Maybe she didn't want to ask you," she countered dryly. Her voice was going fast. At this rate, she soon wouldn't be able to speak at all, she thought grimly.

"Of course she didn't! She's got to be independent. As if it would hurt her to lean on me once in a while." He started to leave the room.

"And who do you lean on?" she asked in a croaky whisper.

Luke turned back, his forehead wrinkled in a frown as he stared at her, brown eyes pensive. "I'm fine," he muttered.

"I see." Darcy shifted in the warm cocoon, feeling the tiredness wash over her in waves. She yawned. "It's all right for you to be independent because you're a big strong man, but it's not for us because we're weak little women. Typical male chauvinist." She snuggled down in her bed and let her eyelids droop, knowing he wouldn't let that comment pass without a rebuttal.

"No one could ever call you weak, Darcy Simms. I don't think I've ever known a stronger woman," he whispered. "Hang onto that inner fortitude, Darcy. You're going to need it around here."

Luke watched as she sighed once and then resumed that steady, even breathing pattern that told him she was asleep. It was true, he decided, staring down at her beautiful face and rich dark hair spread across the pillow. Darcy Simms was one very strong lady. She reminded him a little of Macy, his wife.

Macella Davies had pushed, pulled and dragged him through most of his teenage years. She'd coaxed him to finish school, waited for him while he flirted with a variety of careers, and then quietly advised him to return to ranching.

"It's hard work," she'd laughed up at him. "But that never hurt anyone, did it?" It was a philosophy she'd applied to their married life as well. If there was a job to be done, Macy tackled it head-on. He could still see her in the labor room, face white and strained as she breathed through the contractions.

"Gracious me," she'd puffed, her eyes sparkling with that fire of determination. "This is hard going. They should give women overtime for this." And then she'd dived back into her whooshing as another spasm gripped her body. Luke stuck by her through the whole thing, trying to help in any way he could.

Who had stayed with Darcy? he wondered suddenly, glancing down at the sleeping woman. Macy's labor hadn't lasted more than six hours. He wondered if someone had been there to hold Darcy's hand and encourage her through the various stages until Jamie appeared. Surely she hadn't handled that alone, too?

He shook himself, clenching his teeth in annoyance. What business was it of his what Darcy Simms had done? He wasn't interested in her past—or her future. In fact, once she was better and the will settled, he hoped she'd let him buy her out.

With a twinge of guilt, he remembered Darcy's litany of grief in the graveyard. When she hadn't moved, even after he honked twice, Luke had become concerned about her. Besides he'd lost a wife and child, and understood her feeling of loss.

Martha and Lester, as kind and as sweet as they'd been to him, had somehow never gotten through to Darcy. She still didn't realize that they had missed her so terribly that they'd been willing to go looking for her themselves, and when that was no longer possible, had spent thousands on a private search for her. The physical drain on them had been obvious to him, and he had never doubted that they loved their daughter.

Darcy had sounded bitter and so hurt, as if she were aching for someone to wrap their arms around her and hold her. He knew that feeling. He'd had it the day Macy and Leila had been killed simply because they'd gone to visit a friend in Chicago and been on the wrong street at the wrong time. He'd woken up a happy contented father and gone to bed realizing that his life, as he'd known it, was over.

"Mister Luke?" Jamie stood in the doorway beckoning, his finger to his lips. "Is my mommy all better?"

Luke ruffled the nut-brown hair with a grin and pulled the door almost closed. "Not yet, sport. But she's getting there. She was arguing with me a few minutes ago. Said she wanted to get up." He snickered. "Of course, she fell asleep right after that, so I guess she changed her mind."

"Know what?" the little boy said, "My mom an' me used to play games," he confided with a glint in his eye, changing the subject with a rapidity that Luke was coming to recognize.

"What kind of games?"

"I Spy games. And travel games. We'd put our clothes in a big bag and we'd go on a trip to see a different part of New York. It was fun." The blue eyes sparkled with happy memories.

She'd shielded him, Luke realized. Poor and alone in the huge city, Darcy Simms had managed to protect herself and her son from the ugly side of life. She had absorbed the difficulties of moving from one place to the next to avoid unwanted attention, without him even guessing the reason. Not only that, but she'd given him happy memories. Luke's admiration grew for the feisty woman lying upstairs.

"How would you like to go for a long horseback ride today, Jamie?" Luke found his gloves, plucked two big red apples from the basket on the counter, and grabbed his Stetson.

"Really?" The boy clapped his hands with glee. "Can I have my own horsey?"

Luke burst out laughing at the glow of happiness on the child's face.

"I think we'd better wait to ask your mom's permission for that." He grinned, bending to place a cap on Jamie's head. He hunkered down and quickly slipped off the brown boots, exchanging the right for left. "Today you can ride with me on Thunder. He's very strong, and I'm sure he can carry both of us."

"*Thunder?* Really?" Jamie threw his arms around Luke's neck. "I love you, Mister Luke."

The embrace and the heartfelt emotion behind it threw Luke. He hadn't expected to feel this warm rise of affection for Darcy's son. But as the chubby arms squeezed his neck, Luke realized how much he'd missed losing his daughter so young. His arms came up of their own accord and held the little body tenderly against his chest, experiencing feelings he'd long held in check.

For once in his life, Luke didn't care if he was being sentimental or maudlin. He didn't even allow himself to feel unfaithful to his daughter's memory. He simply stayed where he was and enjoyed the moment for all the joy it held. And then in a voice choked with emotion he murmured, "Thank you."

They spent two hours finding the reluctant cows and directing them, with the help of Shep the dog, back to the rest of the herd. Jamie giggled and laughed and clapped his hands, apparently not feeling the cold as he rode in front of Luke, his excited blue eyes taking in everything.

"I like ranches," he announced as they munched on their apples. "I'm glad I can live here. Can I stay here forever 'n ever, Mister Luke?"

Luke didn't know how to answer the child. If it were up to Luke, Jamie would stay for a very long time, growing stronger and healthier day by day. But that meant Darcy would stay, and Luke wasn't so sure how that made him feel.

He half suspected that before long, she'd be digging out all his secret feelings of betrayal, and he had no stomach for raking over them again. Once he'd had it all...and then he'd lost it. Now there was this ranch to run, Aunt Clarice to take care of, and a future that he'd have to think about. Someday. But not yet.

By the time they returned home, Luke was ready for lunch. He heated some soup for the four of them, and with Jamie's help, made up a tray for the two ladies.

"I didn't give my mom a good-morning kiss," Jamie told him seriously. "She always gets a good-morning kiss or else she can't get up." He put his hand on the edge of the tray in a proprietary manner that made Luke smile. "I can help," he insisted.

Darcy blinked awake as they came into the room, her gorgeous blue eyes widening with joy as she caught sight of Jamie. "Hello, Love Bug!" She helped him up on the bed and accepted his hug with open arms.

"I came to give you the good-morning kiss," he told her seriously. "So you can get up after you eat the lunch me an' Mister Luke made. It's good," he promised, placing a resounding smack on her cheek.

"Thank you, sweetheart." She sipped a bit of soup and nodded. "It's very good. You've done a wonderful job. Have you been a good boy?"

"O' course! She's not getting up yet." Jamie frowned at Luke. "You better give her a good-morning kiss, too."

It was the last thing he'd expected and Luke's startled glance flew to Darcy's. She was beautiful, even after three days in bed with a fever. Her hair flowed away from her face, leaving him with a perfect view of her wide forehead, almond-shaped eyes, thick brown lashes and high, pink-tinged cheekbones. She was blushing, and the sight of it warmed something cold inside Luke.

Her stubborn chin tilted up a fraction as she stared at him. "Jamie, I don't need any more kisses. I'll get up in a little while. Maybe this afternoon. After I have another nap."

"No!" Jamie held his ground. "The daddies have to give the mommies a kiss in the morning. That's the rule."

"Sweetie, Luke isn't your daddy. He doesn't have to kiss me." Darcy's blue eyes darkened with something—what was it? Pain? Remorse?

"He's the daddy in this house," Jamie persisted, his forehead creasing in a frown. He turned to stare at Luke. "You kiss my mommy now, Mister Luke. Then she can get up." He waited patiently.

"Jamie, I told you. Luke isn't—"

"It's all right," he murmured, bending close to Darcy. Luke didn't want to hear the words again. He knew he wasn't a father. Not anymore, at least. But the kid was so intent on getting his mother up. It wouldn't hurt anything, would it?

"There now," he told Jamie, straightening. "Your mommy can finish her lunch and have another nap. Then, maybe, if she feels like it, she could get up for a little while this afternoon. Okay?"

"Yes." Jamie hopped from the bed, almost upsetting the tray in his rush to leave. "We gotta go now, Mom," he explained. "Aunt Clarice needs her good-morning kiss, too. All the ladies in the house get one."

"I see." Luke studied Darcy's rosy cheeks as the child whooped his way back to the kitchen. She looked so young and defenseless sitting there, Luke couldn't help the surge of protectiveness he felt. She didn't deserve the problems she'd had in life.

"I'm sorry." Her husky voice whispered across to him. "He's got a one-track mind at times. Lately it seems to dwell on fathers and their duties."

"It's only natural. Anyway, *I'm* not sorry." Luke grinned down at her with a wink. "He gave me the opportunity to kiss a beautiful woman, and it's barely even noon! I kind of like traditions like that."

If it was possible, Darcy flushed an even deeper shade of pink. Her eyes avoided his as she fiddled with the blankets.

"It's not something I think we should continue," she muttered darkly, peeking up at him quickly before her blue eyes slewed away. "I'm sorry if he's bothering you. I should be able to look after him this afternoon—"

"You can't." Luke didn't even realize he'd said it until he spotted the surprise on her face. "I mean, we planned to go into town this afternoon. I said I'd get him a treat if he behaved this morning—and he did. It's okay, isn't it? He's safe with me, you know. I won't let him out of my sight."

"It's not that," she murmured, looking away from him, her fingers weaving together in agitation. "It's just that, well, I don't want him hurt."

Luke frowned. "No one in Raven's Rest is going to hurt him, Darcy. They probably won't even notice him."

"Oh, they'll notice, all right." She stared up at him piercingly, her eyes blazing with anger. "The illegitimate son of that tramp, Darcy Simms." She mimicked a high-pitched woman's voice. "What a nerve. To dare bring that child back here where decent people are trying to raise their families with values." She clamped her lips together and knotted the sheet, her frustration evident. "That's what they'll say, you know, and I don't want Jamie to hear any of it. My mistakes are not his fault."

"I promise I'll look after him, Darcy. He'll be fine. Can't you trust me?" Luke kept his voice low and soothing. It must be hard to let go, he thought. She'd been alone, fending for herself and the boy for so long that it's natural she finds it hard to release Jamie into someone else's care.

Luke took a step forward, covering her small white hand with his. She started in surprise, but he stayed where he was, his gaze steady.

"I'll watch him as if he were my own," he promised quietly. There was a battle going on in her eyes, one that made him wonder if Darcy Simms had ever really, truly trusted anyone. Her fingers tried to pull away, but Luke held on just enough to let her know that he meant what he said.

Finally she leaned back on her pillows, her eyes closing as she whooshed out a sigh of resignation. Her eyes were darker, more intense, when they opened. They studied his face thoroughly, scrutinizing every detail, before she nodded once.

"All right, he can go. But I'm holding you to your promise."

He smiled. "You won't be sorry, Darcy." With a pang of remorse, Luke suddenly realized just how pale her skin really was.

"Don't worry about supper," he said quietly. "I'll bring something from town." She tried to argue, but Luke cut her off. "Just take it easy today," he ordered brusquely. "Maybe by tomorrow you'll feel like moving around."

He turned to leave, shifting the tray to the side where she could reach it if she needed anything. His glance took in the barely touched soup and the grilled cheese sandwich he'd prepared, now missing only two tiny bites. She'd hardly touched a thing.

"Luke?" He turned at the door and glanced over his shoulder. "Thanks," she whispered, a tiny smile curving her lips.

"You're welcome," he returned, smiling back. "Now get some rest."

"Yes, sir." But it was a playful comment, and he took no offense. After all, how did one argue with a woman who looked like that?

Chapter Eight

Raven's Rest was bustling with folks gathering in town to shop for their annual Thanksgiving supplies. The number of turkeys leaving the grocery store made Luke grin.

"Hey, Luke!" Reverend Anderson slapped him on the back, grinning from ear to ear. "Here to pick up your Thanksgiving supplies, are you? I never knew you could cook."

"I can't, and you know that very well!" Luke smiled back. "But with both Darcy and Clarice laid up, I need a few more TV dinners." He stopped, feeling the tug on his jacket, and glanced down at the little boy hugging his leg. "This is Jamie," he said, lifting the child in his arms.

"Hi, Jamie! My goodness, do you look like your grandmother!" The pastor's booming voice caused the boy to shrink back a little. "She had that same stubborn tilt to her chin."

"I don't gots a grandma," Jamie told him, frowning. "Nor a daddy neither. I just gots my mom and me. An' Mister Luke an' Auntie Clarice," he added after a moment's thought.

"I know." The minister nodded, directing a surprised look in Luke's direction. "But that's a pretty good family to start with, don't you think?" When Jamie nodded, Pastor David turned back to Luke. "What did you say is wrong with the ladies in your house?"

"Darcy's down with a real bad cold," Luke told him, setting the little boy back on the floor and reminding him to stay nearby. "And Aunt Clarice carried a box of clay downstairs and strained her back. We've been nursing them both back to health."

"You? A nurse?" A bubbling laugh burst from the minister. "Somehow, I just can't imagine it," he chortled.

"How about if I round up some folks who'll come out to help with dinner on Thursday? That way your ladies can still get their rest without missing a good meal." He studied the stack of TV dinners in Luke's basket, shook his head, and carefully removed them, shoving them back into the freezer. "No cardboard at Thanksgiving," he muttered, shuddering. "It's against all the rules."

"That would be really nice, David, but I don't know how Darcy would feel about it. She's a little nervous about meeting people."

"Afraid of the gossip, I imagine." The Reverend shook his head, frowning. "Nasty thing, gossip. Never does anything but tear people down. As if anyone wants to be reminded of their past—"

"Reverend Anderson! Surely you're not buying

canned cranberries to go with that turkey I gave you? My word, I didn't think your wife would allow that prepackaged stuff at her table." Ella Lancaster tut-tutted. "Surely you'll be using some of those *fresh* cranberries from the Hansons?"

"I really don't know, Mrs. Lancaster. I'm just following orders."

The Reverend looked a little green around the gills, Luke noted, grinning. "Oh, Reverend Anderson doesn't eat cranberries," he muttered, knowing the old woman would have to make something of it.

"And why not, might I ask? They're very healthy. Clean the gall bladder out wonderfully."

Luke snickered under his breath, wondering how long David could maintain his pasted-on smile. The man had the weakest stomach of anyone Luke had ever known, and the dirty-socks smell of cooking cranberries made him physically ill. Fortunately, Mrs. Lancaster let the subject drop when she spied Jamie.

"Now who is this?" she cooed, chucking the boy under the chin.

Jamie, of course, found sanctuary by hiding himself in Luke's legs, keeping his face firmly hidden. "This is Darcy Simms's son, Jamie," Luke introduced them. "He's a bit shy at the moment."

"Why in the world would he be shy of me?" Ella blurted out. "Come on, boy. Shake hands like a little man."

But Jamie was having none of it. Lifting the boy into his arms, Luke let him keep his chin tucked into his chest.

"How long is she staying?" Ella's mean little eyes

focused intently on Luke. "Looks like she's got you all wrapped up."

"I don't know what you mean." Luke kept his voice low. He wasn't going to stand here with Darcy's son and listen to a lot of innuendo. Neither would he allow her to malign the child's mother over her past.

"Well, you're looking after her kid while she's off doing who knows what!"

Luke heard the pastor suck in his breath as the spiteful words left the woman's mouth. There was a glimmer of sympathy in David's face as he watched Luke get himself under control.

"My mom's sick!" Jamie's little voice broke the tense silence. "She's been in bed for three days. Mister Luke said she's getting better though."

"And how would he know?" Ella demanded, snorting indignantly. "He's a rancher, not a nurse!"

"I called the doctor. He said Darcy had a serious cold. She spent a little too long outside at her parents' grave site." Luke said the words deliberately, reminding the woman of Darcy and Jamie's recent loss.

Luke turned to the minister. "David, would you help Jamie pick out some of those nuts? We're going to have them while we watch a video tonight." He waited till the two were safely out of earshot, his hand reaching out to grasp Mrs. Lancaster's arm before she could scuttle away. "Just a minute. I want to talk to you."

"Let me go."

Luke held his ground. "I will in a minute," he grated. "But first I have something to say to you."

"I imagine it's about bringing something out to the

farm for Clarice," Ella muttered. "I suppose I can take time out of my schedule—for *her*."

Luke shook his head angrily. "Clarice doesn't want your help," he hissed. "And neither do I. Not if you intend to go on maligning Darcy in this way. The ranch is her home, and she has every right to be there."

"She doesn't belong there! Not after the way she's behaved. Look how she ran away and left Lester and Martha to manage on their own. Ungrateful child! Maybe you don't know the grief she caused them, but I do. And then to come home with that, that fatherless boy!" Words seemed to fail her here, and Luke was glad of it. He couldn't listen to any more anyway.

"You don't know anything about it, Mrs. Lancaster. How can you possibly understand what Darcy's life was like, or what made her decide she had to leave? Do you think it was easy for her to manage, alone in the city, with a child?"

"She chose her bed."

"And she's paying for it, if it makes you feel any better," he said. "And I'm sure it does," he muttered under his breath. Luke ached to wipe that smug look off the woman's face. "What gives you the right to go around acting like judge and jury, Mrs. Lancaster? Haven't you ever made a mistake? Or is it just that nobody in Raven's Rest knows about it yet?"

"Of all the nerve!" If the woman didn't vent some of that rage, she was going to burst a blood vessel.

"I quite agree," he muttered grimly. "It takes a lot of nerve to condemn someone you know nothing about, whose problems you couldn't possibly understand. The world would be a whole lot better if people kept their self-righteous noses out of other folks' lives. Good day!'' He turned away and marched down the aisle to find Jamie, rage boiling through his blood.

Was it any wonder Darcy Simms had stayed away from this place for five long years?

"Luke? Luke!'' An urgent hand grabbed his sleeve.

"What? Oh, hi, Jalise.'' He said it apologetically, his eyes busily searching the store. "I'm sorry I didn't see you.''

"I'm not surprised!'' Jalise Penner blinked up at him curiously. "You were stomping away as if something was chewing at your heels.'' She glanced back down the aisle to where Mrs. Lancaster stood frowning, watching them together. "Don't tell me Ella was on your case.''

"Not mine. Darcy's. That woman doesn't have an ounce of humanity in her!''

"Darcy? Darcy *Simms?*'' Jalise's brown eyes sparkled. "You mean she's back? Great!''

Luke searched for some hint of hidden meaning in the words, but Jalise seemed genuinely pleased about the news. "Do you know her?'' he asked carefully, preparing himself for another onslaught.

"Of course I know her. We were in the same class at school. Darcy and I used to be best friends.'' Her eyes clouded. "Until she found someone she preferred more than me.'' Jalise seemed lost in thought for a moment. "How is she?'' she asked at last.

"She's been sick. That's why I brought Jamie along today. Darcy's son, Jamie.''

"I didn't realize she had a son,'' Jalise murmured.

She studied him, her silver-gray eyes speculative. "It doesn't bother you to have him around?"

"No." Luke shook his head, only then acknowledging the truth. "In fact, I've been enjoying Jamie. He's so curious about everything on the ranch."

"Where were they living?"

"New York. This isn't for publication, Jalise, but I'm really glad I found them when I did. I don't know how much longer she could have lasted." He glanced around at the familiar surroundings that he'd begun to take for granted. "The people in this little community have a lot to be grateful for."

When Luke finally caught up with Jamie in the candy aisle, the boy was busily explaining to the minister how they'd moved the cows earlier in the day. His eyes danced merrily, and it was obvious that he hadn't missed Luke one whit.

"All finished your shopping?" Pastor Anderson asked.

"Just about. Thanks, David. Come on, Jamie, my boy. We've got work to do."

Jamie peered up at Jalise, his eyes admiring her white-blond hair. "My name is Jamie Simms," he announced loudly, holding out his hand. "I'm four-and-a-half years old."

"Four?" Jalise stared at him, her eyes darkening as she puzzled that one out. Luke's fears for the boy's sensibilities renewed themselves ten times over before Jalise seemed to get herself under control enough to respond. "Oh. Well, hello, Jamie. My name is Mrs. Penner, but you can call me Jalise. I'm a friend of your mom's." She shook the little hand gravely and gave that smile that Luke had seen soften the hardest heart.

Jamie peered up at her frowning. "My mom don't gots no friends here 'cept Mister Luke and Aunt Clarice. She tol' me."

"Is that right? Well, maybe she forgot about me then. I used to go to school with her, and your mommy was my best friend in the whole world." Jalise seemed to think for a moment and then crouched down beside him. "Do you think you could remember to tell her that I said 'hello'? I'd sure like to visit her when she's feeling better."

"I guess so." Jamie studied her, reaching out one hand to delicately touch the glistening fall of hair. "It's pretty. Do you gots any kids?" he asked quietly.

"No, Jamie, I'm sorry but I don't. I wish I had a little boy like you, though. Your mommy is very lucky."

Luke could hear the tears in her voice. He knew how much it hurt Jalise that she had no child to live on after Billy's death.

"Yes," Jamie agreed in a loud, satisfied voice. "I'm a good boy." He tugged Luke's hand. "Come on, Mister Luke. We gotta go home and look after the pay-shuns." He smiled, delighted with his new word.

"I've got to get going, too," David Anderson told them. "I've got a sermon to prepare for Sunday." He rubbed his chin thoughtfully. "I believe it's time to discuss the Bible's stand on idle gossip."

"Gossip?" Jalise stared at him. "There aren't any scriptures that talk specifically about gossip, are there?"

David winked. "You'll have to come on Sunday to find out, Jalise. See you later."

"Yeah. Thanks, David. I appreciate your... in-

tervention." Luke shook his hand gratefully.

"You're welcome," David chuckled, thrusting his hands in his pockets. He ambled off to his car, his gait slowing again as he approached another parishioner.

"I've got to go, too," Jalise added, glancing at her watch. "I've got Junior Choir tonight." She patted Jamie's head and turned to Luke. "Please tell Darcy to call. I'd love to see her again. It's been too long."

"I'll tell her," Luke promised, but he wanted to tell Jalise not to get her hopes up. Darcy didn't seem willing to allow anyone past the barrier she'd erected, and if Ella Lancaster was any example of the reception she'd receive, he couldn't say he blamed her. "Okay, kiddo!" he said to Jamie. "Let's finish shopping."

By the time Luke got through the checkout and loaded his supplies, the sun was long gone and the wind howled, tossing around stinging bits of icy sleet. He took the road home carefully, grateful for his four-wheel drive, and pulled into the yard with relief.

The warm yellow glow raised his spirits, and he felt a renewed energy course through his veins as he and Jamie lugged the groceries into the house, sniffing appreciatively as the fragrant smell of roasting beef floated out to greet them.

"Something sure smells good," Jamie chirped, tossing off his coat and boots. "My mom musta made something."

Privately, Luke thought so, too, and he was grateful

for it. But he wished she'd taken a little longer to rest. The shadows under her eyes and sunken hollows below her cheeks told him that she needed freedom from stress, sleep, and some decent food to get back to good health.

"Hi, Mom," Jamie squealed, racing across the room to where his mother sat snuggled up on the sofa. "Are you better?"

"Lots better, sweetheart." She accepted his hug readily, returning it with obvious pleasure. "Were you a good boy?" she asked, softly brushing the hair off his forehead.

"Uh-huh. I met a man who works in a church who tol' me I could go there sometimes—if you'd let me—an' see some other kids that come to hear about God. Can I go?"

Luke saw the frown that creased her mouth. "He was talking to David Anderson." He said it quietly, watching for signs that the wall was back up around her once more.

"I meeted a lady, too," Jamie crowed, wiggling away to stand in front of Darcy. "She said she was your friend. I didn't know you had friends here, Mommy."

"Your mom has lots of friends here," Luke told him quietly, flopping into the easy chair. "She used to live here, remember? Jalise and your mom were good friends before your mom had to go away."

Jamie nodded, bent to pick up his airplane from the coffee table and raced from the room, swooping up and down. Luke hoped that the message got through to Darcy: *Not everyone is like Ella Lancaster.*

"You saw Jalise?" Darcy's blue eyes searched his face. "How...how is she?"

"She's lonely. With Billy gone, it's been tough. She tries to fill up her time with meetings and stuff, but I think rattling around in that big old farmhouse must be awfully solitary. She could use a friend."

"I'm sure Billy left her well provided for. He never had a shortage of cash."

Luke gave her a stern look. "Money doesn't buy friends or happiness, Darcy. And the one thing Jalise Penner could use right now is a friend. You were very close once. Maybe you could be again. Why don't you call her?"

"And say what?" Darcy glared at him. "Would you like me to fill her in on my terrible past? Or maybe we could discuss my parents' deaths. That ought to lighten things up!"

"Stop feeling sorry for yourself," he burst out, angry that this woman he was coming to admire couldn't dig herself free of the misery of a past that was dead and gone. "Why don't you try asking her about herself, about some old friends, about her plans? You can give her something no one else can, Darcy."

"I haven't got anything to give. I'm flat broke in case you hadn't noticed." Darcy surged to her feet, the quilt draping around her ankles. "Jalise doesn't need anything from me."

"She needs you to be her friend. That's all. Can't you do that for her?" Luke held her gaze, concern rising as he saw the fear welling up in her eyes, giving her that scared-little-girl look she'd had in New York. She finally broke his stare and tried to move away.

"Sometimes you have to take a chance on people, Darcy," he murmured, gazing down into her expressive eyes, his hands on her narrow waist. "There are some *good* souls out there who will stick with you through thick and thin if you give them a chance."

She made no effort to move away, and frankly, Luke was glad. He enjoyed holding her like this. It had been a long time since he'd felt such a rush of protectiveness flow over him. When she buried her tired head against his chest, he realized how much he'd missed sharing this warmth and closeness with someone.

"I'd like to believe in your pipe dream, Luke," she whispered. "I really would. But reality is a whole different ball game. I know what the people here think of me. I've known it all along. And I don't care." There was a tinge of loneliness to that statement that made it ring false.

"I think you're a strong beautiful woman who's taken on life determined to prove a point." He let his arms tighten around her just a fraction. "You've proven it, Darcy. You can handle what you're given. But doesn't it get lonely doing it all by yourself?"

She dropped her hands from his chest. "That's the only way I know *how* to handle things."

"You aren't alone. God is there, waiting for you to lean on Him. If you want to." He stared into her eyes. "I'm here, too." Luke met her gaze. "If you want me," he added softly, unsure himself of exactly what he meant. All he knew was that she was hurting and he wanted desperately to help, to take it away. To make her world good and happy again.

"I guess I *could* use a friend."

The whisper-soft words brushed over his skin as she spoke, her pink lips tantalizing him. It was inevitable that he would kiss her. As a friend he wanted to reassure her, to ease the load a little. But as his mouth brushed across hers and she returned his kiss, Luke mentally admitted the truth. Darcy Simms touched his heart in a way that had nothing at all to do with sympathy. And from her response, Luke was pretty sure that he'd moved up a step from interloper-ranch hand. Which was a good thing.

Wasn't it?

Chapter Nine

"Miss Ridgely? I was wondering if you still had that job of teacher's aide open? I'd like to apply for it." Darcy forced a note of calmness into her voice and ignored the twenty or so other people in the staff room who sat peering at her.

"Yes, dear, I have. And the job hasn't been filled. Oh, it will be lovely to have an extra set of hands around here! Come with me, Darcy. I'll just get the forms from my desk. I was hoping you'd be back." The benevolent smile of the older woman sent Darcy's spirits soaring.

The few early-bird students that had already arrived were still outside playing in the newly fallen snow. Darcy could hear their cries and giggles through the huge glass windows in Miss Ridgely's room.

"This is wonderful news, Darcy. I just know you'll be so good at this job. It's too bad you didn't go on to college. You would make a wonderful teacher."

It was the second time she'd heard it in as many

weeks, and Darcy couldn't help but wonder if she would be any use as a teacher. In New York it *had* been she who had shown the other girls the routine— that was true. And she did enjoy explaining things. But teaching? That was a whole different ball game.

"Here we are." Hilda held the form up triumphantly.

"You're sure you think I can do this?" Darcy studied the woman's shining eyes. "I've never tried anything like it before, but it *is* interesting."

"Darcy, you're a natural teacher. You have an innate ability to hear all the things people don't say. That's going to stand you well when you deal with these children. I wish you'd think more about taking those distance courses. It wouldn't take you that long, and you could really have a good basis to work on your degree."

"I don't think I could afford college," Darcy told her, feeling a private sense of loss. "Not with Jamie, and helping out on the farm."

"But you don't have to pay for it all at once. It's not as if you'd be taking a full load."

"No, but it still means money. How much is a full-credit course now?"

"They vary, naturally, but I happen to have a calendar here..." Hilda held it out so Darcy could see the fee structure.

"I could probably afford that," Darcy began doubtfully, "but the work might be beyond me." Still, the dream of herself in a classroom tantalized her.

"Of course you could do it. With your hands tied!" Hilda's voice was refreshingly reassuring, and in the face of such enthusiasm, Darcy couldn't help but grin back.

"I don't know. It seems like such a big project. And I can't guarantee just how long Luke will continue with this arrangement. He might decide he wants to move on somewhere else." Or that he wants me gone, she admitted to herself.

"That's the beauty of distance education. Doesn't matter where you are. And I'd be happy to have you in my class to do your internship."

Darcy couldn't help it—she was catching this positive spirit. "I can't thank you enough, Hilda. This will be so wonderful."

"Yes, it will. I enjoy my classes each day, but it will be so nice to have someone to share them with. I wonder…" She tapped the tip of her nose as her thick bushy eyebrows drew together. "You may be able to claim some of the time you spend as an aide as a credit—apprenticeship or something. I'll check into that." She made a note to herself and stuck it on the side of her filing cabinet.

"Um, Miss Ridgely?" Darcy wondered just how to word a touchy question. "I was wondering, that is, well, what about Annette? I know she doesn't really want me here. Mostly because of the past, but still, I don't want to make things uncomfortable for you."

"Annette's stubborn, but she's talked to the board and they feel that you should be given a chance at the position. Since we're so short of help, she can hardly object." Hilda patted her shoulder comfortingly. "Don't worry about Annette, Darcy. Just concentrate on the task before you."

"I will," Darcy promised. "Now, would you like to show me what I'll be working on if I get the job?"

"God is more than a judge to His children."

Reverend Anderson's topic for a sermon struck Darcy as unusual. Everyone knew that God judged people for their sins. And goodness knew, she had a pile of sins to make up for. Everyone knew that, too.

"It's not that He doesn't know we've done wrong. And it's not that He doesn't care." The pastor's face was alive with the excitement of his faith as he spoke to the congregation packed into the tiny church. "But God is not like human beings. He doesn't dwell on someone's mistakes, hashing and rehashing them over and over, always standing in judgment even after we've asked His forgiveness. God says that once you've repented of the wrong, He remembers it no more…"

Several people in front of Darcy shifted uneasily in their seats. She felt particularly uncomfortable herself. Perhaps it was the heat; so many people crowded into such a small area was bound to make it warmer than usual. It was funny, though. Clarice didn't seem to notice it. Nor did Luke, who sat facing the front with Jamie comfortably seated on his lap.

"…As members of God's family, can we do less than God does? Can we afford to hang onto the past and constantly harangue ourselves and others about it? Isn't it time we faced up to our shortcomings and got on with the life we've been given today?"

There wasn't a sound in the sanctuary. Not a single baby cried, not one teenager shifted. Every eye was focused on the man standing behind the pulpit, speaking a truth so painful that it hurt the listeners to hear.

"The Bible tells us not to judge anyone, lest we ourselves be judged by the same harsh measure. Dearly beloved, is that how you want to spend your time, criticizing everyone who has made a mistake?" His voice dropped. "Then you'd better start your judgments by looking in the mirror. *Let the one who is blameless cast the first stone.*"

Darcy glanced down at her hands, shamed by her own judgmental attitude toward the people who sat in front of her and behind her. If she had a bad reputation, there was a reason, wasn't there? She'd deliberately played the part of town brat and fed into people's impressions. What goes around comes around, she reminded herself bitterly.

"My dear family, our heavenly Father is concerned with the future of His children. He wants us to get beyond all the pain and mistakes of the past. God wants to move into the future and show us such hope and joy, we can't imagine it. Forget the hurts and the disappointments. Put them away."

The words floated around Darcy's head. So easy to say, she thought sadly. So difficult to do.

"The past cannot be changed, dear ones. It's dead and gone. But we have a whole new canvas in front of us. We can paint whatever we wish on that. Choose!" Everyone sat straighter, startled by the peremptory command.

"Choose right now whether you will make your life a picture of joy, happiness and sharing, or whether you will drag all the old ugly disappointments of the past onto that pristine blank page and dirty it up with what God has already forgotten. He's given you the opportunity to sparkle and shine. Will you ignore that and rust away in your past?''

Darcy stood with the rest of the congregation and halfheartedly sang the words to the closing hymn. The pastor's words rang in her head as she shook hands with a few old friends—and walked past those who turned their backs.

"Good sermon." Clarice shook the Reverend's hand vigorously. "Right to the point. Top-notch."

"Thank you, Clarice. I only hope it sinks in."

"Takes a while. A body needs to meditate on the right path. Better not to make quick decisions."

"Yes, you're absolutely right." David Anderson grinned in satisfaction. "So many people just let the days roll by without realizing that they won't get a second chance. How's your back?"

"Still there," Clarice quipped, her prim mouth stretched wide. "Been getting lots of walking in. Helps." She nodded once and then marched down the steps to the group of ladies huddled on the lawn.

"Darcy. How are you? I understand you've also been ill." There was sympathy in those eyes, as if they saw everything that was in her heart, and understood.

"Just a cold. I'm fine now, thanks to Luke." She sent a smile his way.

"Well, that's good to hear. And I'm very happy you came this morning." Pastor Anderson squeezed her hand. "Very glad."

"I'm afraid that's due to Luke, too. He's awfully hard to say 'no' to! Not that I wanted to," she amended with a blush. "Not after everyone was so kind about Thanksgiving. That was a lovely meal you brought out. Clarice and I could never have managed it in our conditions. And Luke isn't exactly…handy when it comes to cooking.''

Darcy couldn't help the smile that tickled the corner of her lips at the sight of the frown on Luke's handsome face. He'd been adamant that she had to make a public appearance today, especially after the townsfolk had driven out with a wonderful array of turkey, ham and all the fixings. But Darcy hadn't missed the four TV dinners he'd secreted at the back of the freezer. When the pastor arrived at the farm, she'd deliberately heated them up for lunch yesterday. His dour look now reminded her that he wasn't going to let it slide.

Still, in spite of feeling uncomfortable during the service, and even though she knew all the old hens were cackling even now, Luke had been right about this service, she conceded. In spite of everything, she was glad she had come, if only to listen to the lovely music.

''See. You lived! Next time, don't bother arguing,'' Luke murmured in her ear as they went out the door. ''It wasn't that bad, was it?''

''Bad enough. I felt like every pair of eyes in the place was staring at me for a while. Thank goodness the junior choir had that presentation.'' Darcy watched as Jamie spoke to some children racing around the parking lot. The other kids seemed to accept him for what he was—a little boy who wanted to make friends. She heaved a sigh of relief as her son joined the group.

''Dar, is that you?'' Jalise Penner raced down the

stairs in the most unladylike fashion and stopped in front of Darcy, panting. "You haven't changed a bit. Welcome home!"

Darcy found herself wrapped in welcoming arms and hugged for all she was worth. She couldn't do any less than return the greeting as her eyes filled with tears.

"Thank you, Jay," she said at last, holding the other woman at arm's length. "It's nice to be back...I guess."

"Oh, the old tabbies have been having a go, I suppose?" Jalise glanced from Luke to Darcy and then back to Luke, who inclined his head. "Forget about them," she advised, glaring at Mrs. Lancaster as the woman stared rudely and then leaned over to whisper in her neighbor's ear.

"Remember, Dar, this is Raven's Rest. They have to talk about something other than—"

"—the weather, crop prices and Joe Blow's new haircut," Darcy finished with a grin. She burst out laughing at Jalise's pained look.

"At least it takes their tongues off me." Jalise pitched her voice in a loud, rather squeaky tone that Darcy was sure would be heard by the other women. "That girl needs a man and a passel of children," she cackled. "Billy shouldn't have left her with so much time on her hands. Why she's wearing herself out with that café!"

Jalise reverted to her normal tones. "As if he just wandered off without thinking that he was going for good and I might want a child before he left. Honestly! But you know, Dar, I think what bugs me more than their nasty gossiping is that they call my lovely, wonderful restaurant a café! Even though I specifically called it The Coffee Klatsch.''

"Luke told me about Billy. I'm so sorry, Jalise.'' Darcy hugged her old friend once more. "How are you managing?''

"I'm okay. I've had some time to deal with it and even though I wish he'd hung around for a little longer, I can't wish him back. God has a plan. I know that.'' She grimaced. "I just don't know what it is.''

"Join the club.'' Darcy studied the face she'd known so well. It was thinner now, older. Sadder. But then, weren't they all?

"Why don't you drop in for coffee some afternoon?'' Jalise invited. "I usually take off between two and four. I've been needing someone to confide in.''

Darcy was so relieved that Jalise didn't want to talk about the past that she agreed to meet her friend for coffee the next day. "I have to see the lawyer anyway,'' she murmured with a telling glance at Luke. "I want to know how things stand.''

"Well, Old Man Pettigrew is back home, so that'll probably work out,'' Jalise agreed. "If you're looking for something to do, I can always use someone to help out in the *café*.'' She grinned playfully.

"Oh, Jay! That's so kind of you. And thank you. But I'm going to start as a teacher's aide and I don't want to be away from Jamie too much right now. Next year he'll be in school you know.''

"Yes, I know.'' There was a strange note in Jalise's voice that Darcy was afraid to analyze. "You are so lucky. He's a wonderful little boy.''

"Yes, he is,'' Luke put in softly. "And if we don't

get him out of that snowbank, he'll probably freeze to death. You girls can chitchat all you like, but I'm getting Jamie and we're going to the truck. I'm not needed here anyway!''

Darcy burst out laughing at his mock offended expression, and heard Jalise join her. Together they watched Luke coax Jamie away from his friends and into the cab.

"I guess that's a hint," Darcy mumbled. "I see Clarice is already sitting in the back. I'd better go."

"See you tomorrow. And be prepared to hang around. We've got a lot to catch up on." Jalise waved at Luke before scurrying across the lot to her own little car.

As Darcy strode over to the truck, her mind whirled with the activities of the morning. It hadn't been nearly as bad as she'd feared. No one had said anything out of the ordinary, and some folks had certainly gone out of their way to make her feel welcome.

Maybe Clarice and the good minister were right, she reflected. Maybe this was a new beginning and maybe—just maybe—she could start over again. She resolved to put the past behind her, and then wondered exactly how one went about doing that. Especially when one had a four-year-old reminder of exactly what the past entailed.

Chapter Ten

"Don't envy me, Jay. It really wasn't all that glamorous. While you were here getting married, I was scrounging for my next meal and dodging every lecher in the city!"

Jalise reached out and squeezed her hand. "I'm sorry you had to go through all that, Darcy. And I'm sorry that I wasn't there for you. Not that you needed me. Not with God on your side. Besides, you're very strong, you know. It's something I've come to admire about you."

"Really? I guess I've never thought of myself as being particularly strong. Rebellious maybe, but not strong." Darcy fidgeted in her chair. "I suppose you know about the ranch?"

"You mean about Luke inheriting half?" Jalise nodded. "In this kind of place you can't avoid the gossip, and much as I hate to admit it, there's usually some part of it that's true. Are you upset?"

"I was at first. Furious. But then I realized that my

parents probably just wanted to protect their lifelong work. And I wasn't around to see to it. Luke was here—he was like their son. He has a right to whatever they wanted him to have. I don't really deserve anything.''

"Of course you do, Darcy! Don't sell yourself short, kid. You do know your parents tried to find you? Your dad spent a lot of time chasing down leads. That's why he needed Luke. Then, of course, he got sick and he couldn't spend as much time as he wanted to. But for a while there, Lester and Martha would take off every weekend, driving here and there to find out if anyone had any news about you.''

That was the last thing Darcy'd expected to hear, and she could hardly believe it. "They tried to find me?''

"Of course they did, Dar! They were worried about you when you didn't answer their ads.''

"I never saw any ads,'' Darcy murmured, staring at her. "But then, I didn't have much money for newspapers, either.'' She frowned. "Jay, I can't quite believe this. You're saying that my parents actually tried to find me and get me to come home?''

Jalise nodded. "But after your dad got so sick, the doctor told him he had to take it easy, stop worrying. By then your mom couldn't do much more. I used to go out and see them quite often. To cheer them up, you know?'' Darcy closed her eyes, trying to absorb all this information. "I think if Luke hadn't coerced Clarice into coming here and shaking things up, your mother would have just given up. Clarice convinced them to forget about what they couldn't fix and concentrate on what they could.''

"And that's when the air-conditioning and new appliances came in?" Darcy guessed, watching Jalise closely.

"Uh-huh. It wasn't that they forgot about you, Darcy. They had to do something for someone else or go crazy with guilt."

"Guilt?" Darcy whispered the word, somehow afraid to hear what Jalise would say next.

"They felt a terrible guilt. Your mother told me once that she'd been given a gift from God when you were born and that she had only just realized that she had messed things up by trying to make you perfect. It took your leaving for her to see that she'd ruined that gift."

"You can't *make* a child do anything. Not in the long term. You can only teach them and care for them and let them know how much they mean to you." Darcy whispered the words as she stared at her hands. "Jamie taught me that. He's my child and I love him more than life. I have hopes and dreams for him— but I don't own him. He is his own little person."

Jalise nodded. "I know. You seem like a great mother. But it was a lesson that it took your mom so long to learn, maybe because of her own childhood. I don't know. But she always thought you knew how much she loved you, Dar."

"She never said it—not once that I can remember." Darcy hunched over in her chair and stared at her friend. "I *ached* to hear them say that, and they never did."

"Are you sure, honey?" Jalise wrapped her long slim fingers around Darcy's arm and squeezed. "Are you sure they never said it? Sometime when you're alone and have time, try to remember more than the rotten times. I think you'll find that your parents tried to tell you in a hundred different ways that they loved you.''

Somehow Darcy managed to get through the next few minutes without bawling. But later, as she walked down the street toward the church, her mind flew back to a past she would rather forget. Had there really been love there, and she'd missed it?

''Darcy, good morning. I hope you're feeling well.''

''I'm fine, Reverend Anderson. And thank you again for the wonderful Thanksgiving feast. I don't know how you managed to get so much into your car. I hope it wasn't damaged from the trip,'' she teased.

''You know how those dents got in the side, don't you? A turkey leg popped out and struck an oncoming vehicle.'' His face was perfectly serious, and Darcy couldn't help smiling. ''Actually, I was hoping I'd meet you. I wanted to ask you something.''

''Go ahead,'' Darcy said.

''It's about the Christmas pageant. Jalise Penner will be leading the junior choir while the rest of the Sunday School students are putting on a play.''

''Sounds lovely.'' She kept her voice carefully noncommittal.

''Actually, it's a pretty good way to make sure no children are left out. Not everyone can be counted on to recite a poem or a story. But with the music and just a few recitations, I think we can make it an evening of praise and worship to the King.''

''I'm sure it will be wonderful.''

''The thing is, we haven't any costumes. René

Jones did design a few things, and Bettina Bensen donated the fabric from her store, but no one has time to sew them up. And those who are willing simply don't have the expertise needed to translate René's ideas into reality."

"And you hoped I'd be able to help out?" Darcy finished for him, wondering if the whole world knew that she'd been working in the garment district. "Ordinarily I would. I'm sure René's costumes are wonderful. But I've just agreed to take on the teacher's aide position at school, and I said I'd help Luke with the ranch bookkeeping. I don't think I'd have time for anything more." She felt a pang of regret and wondered why it was suddenly important to her to do this.

"The pageant isn't until Christmas Eve, Darcy. And we don't need the costumes until right before that. Isn't there some way you could manage it?" He sounded so earnest that Darcy found herself reconsidering. "I'm sure Jalise would help. René might even be talked into lending a hand. Please?"

Darcy frowned. She didn't owe these people anything. The past was gone and she intended to focus on the future as Clarice had suggested. So why did she feel somehow beholden?

"It's a big night for Jalise," Reverend Anderson continued softly. His eyes glowed with some inner secret. "She's been planning this for months."

Three days later Darcy had to bite her lip to keep from rescinding her silly offer to help. Mounds of white gauzy "angel" fabric sat waiting for the scissors. There were rich velvets for the wise men, bark cloth for the shepherds, and wooly "sheepskins" to be shaped and stuffed with wriggling little boys and girls.

"Why do I let you get me into these things, Jalise?" Darcy moaned as her friend quickly shaped wings from wire coat hangers. "We'll never get through all of this!"

"Oh, don't be such a pessimist! These are only for the manger scene. The rest of the play uses everyday clothes."

"Yes, but look at these sketches! They're so elaborate." Darcy spread the drawings over the huge cutting table in the seniors' center, studying them with a groan. "I don't know how to make patterns for this headgear!"

"So, let's call René and get her to come over and show us." Jalise walked to the phone and dialed before Darcy could object.

Five minutes later René was explaining the historical significance of the garments and how each would fit the actor.

"You must know a little about this stuff, Darcy. You worked in a clothing outfit in New York, didn't you?" An envious note crept into René's otherwise dull voice. "Surely you got to see them design the patterns?"

"Yes, I did. But I never had to translate pattern to fabric. I usually worked in other areas." Darcy forced herself to remain calm and unruffled. "I heard that you won yourself a pretty prestigious place at Chelan's. I envy you that. They've got some of the best designs in the city."

"Yeah, I did. But I never got to finish it out. That's been a regret of mine."

"I know what regret is like," Darcy commiserated. "I have a few of those myself."

"It's weird, really. When you're eighteen, you're ready to take on anyone and anything and you think you have all the time in the world. And then one day you wake up and find out that your window of opportunity has vanished, that it's all over and you've missed your chance."

"You haven't missed anything, René," Jalise burst out. "You've got a wonderful husband, a nice home, a beautiful daughter. Some women would kill for that."

"I'm not 'some women.'" René's voice was full of hurt, and Darcy suddenly felt compassion for the vivacious redhead. "To me, Raven's Rest is the end of the earth."

"I know what you mean," Darcy murmured, thinking of her own situation. "When I left here, I was full of plans for the future. I wasn't going to even come back until I could show my parents that I didn't need them."

"I only ever wanted to stay here with Billy and raise my family." Jalise stared at the quilt hanging on the wall as tears formed at the corners of her eyes. "I thought I'd done all the right things and yet still I didn't get my heart's desire...."

They worked steadily, quietly. Darcy organized each pattern piece with the others until she had three complete wise men outfits. René started on the shepherds' costumes, and Jalise continued to wrap white gauze around the angel's wings she'd formed.

"It sort of makes me think of this," Jalise said after a long contemplative silence. When the others frowned at her, she grinned and waved a hand at the mess surrounding them. "Well, look at this chaos! Someone who walked in would think that there isn't rhyme or reason to what we're doing. René's just hacking away at that, and you're picking up her left-overs."

"And?" René slit a neckline in the sheep's head.

"I know what she means." Darcy grinned. "It might look like a mess, but actually we *are* organized and there *is* a method to what we're doing."

"Exactly!" Jalise beamed with satisfaction.

"So what?" retorted René. "How does that help me know what to do with this craving I have? It doesn't. This omnipotent plan you're so infatuated with is Greek to me. I can't see the point of it. Why couldn't Jesse's father have found someone else to run his ranch? Why did we have to come back here?" There were tears in her beautiful eyes.

"You really mean, why did Ginny have to be born with her disease?" Jalise added softly, and patted the slim shoulder as René burst into fresh tears. "I don't know the answer to that, sweetheart. Nobody does. But it's what we've got to work with."

"I don't *want* to work with it. I want things to be the way I want them."

Darcy smiled to herself at the tone of rebellion in René's voice. It sounded like her own voice, she decided grimly. René was saying exactly what Darcy had felt for years. And the answer that she was getting wasn't any more satisfactory to her than the one Darcy had come up with for her own situation.

"The thing is, René—" Jalise's forehead furrowed in thought "—we don't know how your ideas would have worked out either. We know what we want to happen, but maybe that wouldn't have been the case either. Maybe if you'd stayed at in-training, you wouldn't have had Ginny. Or maybe Jesse would have been hurt or gotten mixed up in something evil. We just don't know.''

''Or maybe everything would have gone along perfectly, and I'd be set up as a designer right now, showing the world my creations.'' René's lips tightened.

''And I'd have gone to school and gotten a really good job somewhere with people who cared about me,'' Darcy added.

''And maybe I'd have six children by now and be happily at home, raising them! It's useless to 'what if' all the time. It didn't happen—and we have to get on with what *did*.''

''How?'' René glared at the others fiercely. ''By pretending that what we really want doesn't matter? It matters, Jalise. It hasn't just gone away.''

''And it won't. God made you the way you are, honey. He doesn't want you to deny the very desires that He's given you. He just wants you to find a new way to use them.''

''And what about Darcy?'' Darcy wanted to know the answer herself.

''I don't know what God's plans are,'' Jalise admitted. ''I'm just speculating that if we didn't go down one trail, maybe it's because God meant for us to do something else. Maybe Darcy had to come home to face her demons before she can move on.''

''And you?'' Darcy studied her friend's thoughtful look. ''What do you see as God's reason for your situation? Didn't He want you and Billy to be married? Is that why Billy died?''

"No! Billy and I were meant to be together. I knew that from long ago. And we did have a wonderful married life. But it wasn't all pain free. We disagreed on a lot of things. And Billy suffered terrible bouts of depression. It wasn't all roses, you know.''

"So what's the point?'' René frowned. "What's the reason?''

"I don't know,'' Jalise repeated. "I just know that I'm supposed to pick up the pieces and go on. Billy's and my dreams of a family are gone. But I'm still here, and I'm alive. I have to wait for God to show me the next step.''

"All I have to say is that it's pretty frustrating!'' René gathered up the scraps and shoved them into a garbage bag.

"That's for sure,'' Darcy agreed grimly. "I no more wanted to come back here than fly to the moon. It's been really hard to deal with all the nasty remarks and speculation. People wondering about Jamie, talking about him. What good does that do me?''

"It's made you stronger, for one thing.'' Jalise's silver-gray eyes sparkled. "The old Darcy would have retaliated if someone dared to say something she didn't like. Remember those eggings you carried out so frequently? The old Darcy would have tried to get back at anyone who got on her wrong side. You've grown beyond that because you faced the past.''

"And I've seen you with Luke Lassiter several times lately,'' René added with a gleam in her eye. "The two of you seem pretty cozy. I remember a time when you wouldn't let anyone but Josiah Pringle within forty feet of you." She grinned. "I guess that's all changed if that kiss you and Luke exchanged in the park yesterday was any indicator."

Darcy flushed, studying her fingers. "It was just a thank-you kiss," she murmured. "He helped me get all the papers in for a course I'm taking. It didn't mean anything." But she knew she was lying. It meant quite a lot to her to be held in those strong arms and treated like someone special, someone who mattered.

"No, of course not. How silly of me! Didn't mean anything, my foot!" René smirked. "So that's why Luke's been floating on air for days on end. I knew he liked you, of course. But I only half speculated that he was interested in you romantically, too."

"He's not! We're just…friends." Darcy searched for an out; whatever was between her and Luke was too new to bear this scrutiny. "He's just been helping me."

Jalise looked at René, who nodded her red head smugly. "Uh-huh." They grinned happily. "Friends—*right*."

"Oh, for pity's sake!" Darcy packed up her fabric pieces and, with the others' help, loaded them into Clarice's little car. But as she drove home, she considered in a whole new light her relationship with the tall dark cowboy.

Luke was not like any man she'd ever known. He didn't pay any attention to what other people thought, for one thing. He just went ahead and did what he felt was right. Jamie was no relation and yet the man had tucked the child under his protective wing by introducing him to all the wonders of the ranch.

They'd spent hours talking about the livestock, the land and the jobs that needed doing, when Luke must have longed for some peace and quiet.

"You can do this," he'd encouraged her when she stood trembling in front of the distance education building in Denver. "You're smart, you know what's important and you love children. You'll make a wonderful teacher." And with those words ringing in her ears, she'd walked into that building and answered hundreds of questions without the least bit of hesitation. She'd even had enough spunk to ask for concessions and—wonder of wonders—the faculty head had agreed to give her credit for her hours of aide work.

Darcy steered the car through town and out onto the highway.

"Is there really some point to this coming home business?" she asked herself, thinking of Jalise's words. "Has it all been part of some master plan?"

Clarice's words from the battered, worn Bible that she insisted on reading out loud every morning came back. *"The Lord longs to be gracious to you; He rises to show you compassion."*

"Why would God show me compassion? What am I to Him?"

Like the fluttering wing of a dove, the answer flew straight to her heart and landed there with assurance. She was God's child. He cared about her!

"I didn't know," she whispered in awe, staring at the darkness that surrounded her. "I didn't know that You were there, worrying about me."

Suddenly Clarice's words made sense. God hadn't abandoned her. He'd just let her go off on her own tangent for a while. Hadn't she done the same thing with Jamie when he'd been dead set on doing things his own little way? Wasn't that a way of educating him, just as her own self-centered journey had taught her much about life?

"Why did the bug die, Mommy?" She remembered his dismay when he'd insisted on keeping the worm in his pocket.

"Because worms can't live in pockets. They need soil and light and air. I told you that, remember?"

"But I want it to live, Mommy!"

Darcy suddenly accepted that she had been acting like Jamie—demanding that God rearrange things to suit her instead of seeing that there was a better path to follow. If she had only let go of the anger and the doubt a year ago and come back sooner, maybe she'd have seen her parents one last time....

Darcy pulled into the yard, but sat with the motor running, staring up into the night sky. *I'm sorry,* she whispered brokenly. *I've done it all wrong. I didn't know, didn't understand. I'll try to do better. I'll listen before judging. I'll pay more attention. I'll get it right somehow. I can do this. I can make up for the past.*

And feeling more confident than she had in days, Darcy hurried into the house, intent on Christmas, Luke, Clarice and Jamie. The future. Their future.

Chapter Eleven

"Something smells wonderful," Luke said, his nose in the air, sniffing.

Darcy smiled as she lifted a pan from the oven. Two weeks till Christmas and she was worse than Jamie. She could hardly wait to enjoy everything.

"It's Christmas cookies. Mommy an' me are baking cookies and butter tarts." Jamie's face was covered with an assortment of flour, cookie dough and icing. "See, I made an angel." He held up a crooked little figure with distended wings and a halo that had bent down over one eye.

"It's a very pretty angel, too." Luke smiled, his eyes meeting Darcy's with a question. "Why is it purple?"

"'Cause I like purple. An' they told us at Sunday School that when people wore purple in the Bible it was 'cause they were royal. This is a royal angel." He sounded slightly offended that Luke hadn't known.

"Yes, now that you mention it, I can see that," Luke agreed solemnly. "Can I have one to eat?"

"No!" Jamie looked shocked at the very idea. "These are for Christmas."

"But sweetheart, we have lots. I think Luke could have just one, don't you? After all, we let Clarice taste one." Darcy had to look away from the admiring glow in Luke's dark brown eyes, hoping he would assume the flush on her cheeks was from the oven. "I just warmed some mulled cider if you'd like to try it. It was my mother's favorite recipe."

"Mulled cider?" He shook his head. "I don't think I've ever had it. But I'm willing to try some." He sat down at the end of the table, waiting patiently while Jamie chose just which cookie he should have.

Darcy poured a bright red-and-green mug full of the steaming cinnamon-scented drink, her heart pounding a little faster as she set it before him. His fingers brushed hers and from the glow in his eyes, Darcy was pretty sure the touch was no accident.

"Thank you," his low voice whispered in her ear as she straightened.

Darcy smiled back shyly. "You're welcome."

"Here. You can have this one. It's got its wing broked." Jamie handed over the damaged cookie, and watched soberly as Luke's white teeth bit into the glossy red icing.

"Why didn't you give him one of the better ones?" Darcy asked, studying the head bent so seriously over the table. "When we give someone something, we always want to give them the best and keep the broken ones for ourselves," she lectured, wondering if he was too young to understand.

"But, Mommy!" Jamie protested indignantly. "You said they all taste the same, whether they have a bit missing or not!"

"He's got you there." Luke's laughing voice was for her ears alone, and Darcy grinned back. "Anyway, we have to keep the really special ones for when people come to visit us, right, Jamie? We don't want our company to eat broken cookies."

Our company. It sounded so...familial. As if they were a cohesive group working together. A family. It was surprising just what a warm glow spread to her heart at those offhanded words of Luke's.

"How about if you and I build a snowman, Jamie? The snow's just wet enough that it might stand up overnight."

"Yes!" Jamie jumped down from his chair and rushed to the bathroom to wash his sticky hands.

"He sure moves," Luke chuckled. "Energy to burn."

"Don't I know it!" Darcy swept up the flour from the floor, then set about scrubbing the table. "He's got icing everywhere."

She could feel Luke watching her, and it made her strangely nervous; she had to pay special attention when removing the last pan of cookies. Then, with a deft movement, she slipped in two pans of butter tarts and reset the timer.

"Do you have anything special planned tonight?" he asked.

She turned to find his eyes fixed on her, his mouth tilted upward at one corner in a secretive smile. "I've got an assignment due on Thursday that I should do a little more work on."

"I thought you said you'd finished that. And I know you've done the books up to date because I checked. Can't you take just a few hours off? You'll enjoy it, I promise."

His words were so persuasive and his eyes so hopeful that Darcy couldn't have denied him even if she'd wanted to. And she didn't want to.

"What time?"

"Oh, after supper. Clarice and Jamie can come, too."

Now why did that disappoint her? Darcy wondered. She loved her son and Clarice, too! But it would have been nice if Luke had asked to spend just a little while alone with her.

Darcy forced herself to think of supper, and cleaned the kitchen with enough elbow grease to make it sparkle. Once she had the chicken potpies cooking, the potatoes roasting and the table set, she wasted a few moments peering out the window to where Luke and Jamie were building their snowman.

They look so good together. Like a *real* father and son, her mind whispered as she watched Luke help Jamie lift the head onto the snowman. Luke was patient and gentle, even when Jamie grew cranky and tired. And despite the boy's constant questions, Luke managed to teach him with a calm understanding and forbearance that Darcy found sadly lacking in herself at times.

And Clarice was the perfect grandmother for Jamie. She didn't seem to mind when he crawled up on her lap with sticky hands, spilled his milk on her best shoes, or cut up the catalog she'd ordered specially from the pottery store. She read him Bible stories constantly and expanded on their principles by using ordinary everyday events that seemed to stay in his little mind long after the story had been forgotten.

In fact, both of the Lassiters had been a godsend, and Darcy found herself asking "why" less and less. It may not have seemed like it at one time, but this was indeed her *home*. And she was happy to be here in spite of all the bad memories that she had once held. Now, inch by inch, day by day, she was building new memories with Clarice and Luke.

She felt confident about the decision she'd made to put her trust in God and His plans. And somehow, with the acceptance of that decision, all of the terrible bitterness and hate that she had carried for so long was slowly but surely ebbing away.

"He loves that little boy." Clarice's voice came over her left shoulder. "We both do. It's going to be a wonderful Christmas. It's been so long since I've had a little one to watch and fuss over."

"You fuss over him too much." Darcy grinned, slipping her hand into Clarice's. "He's going to be spoiled rotten." And she didn't mind in the least.

"Nonsense. He has far too much character for that. And he's been so good for Luke. I know the boy hasn't said much, but Jamie fills a hole in his heart that's been aching for a long time. Ever since Leila and Macy died."

Leila and Macy. Now, at last, Darcy had names for the two people who haunted Luke's past. She felt sorry they'd gone; sorry that she never knew them. But she was glad if Luke took a little comfort from her son. After all, he'd already given them so much.

The buzzer rang, signaling the readiness of the biscuits. While Clarice went to call the others in, Darcy lifted out the golden-brown rolls. She'd worked especially hard to make this meal—one of Luke's favorites—extra festive. And judging by the gleam in his warm brown eyes, she'd succeeded.

"Wow! All of my favorites. I'm a lucky man, Jamie, my boy. Thank you, Darcy. This is wonderful." He never failed to compliment her on her cooking, and Darcy couldn't help the little glow that bubbled up inside. It was nice to be appreciated.

"They're all *my* favorites, too." Jamie eagerly helped himself to one of the biscuits. He dropped it quickly as Clarice bowed her head, following her lead and waiting for Luke to say grace: "Father, we thank You for Your bounty to us. And we thank You for the season of Your son's birth. Thank You for sending Him to take our punishment. Help us to be a blessing to others. Amen."

"Amen," Jamie added loudly, and then made sure all eyes were open before buttering his biscuit.

The four of them enjoyed a lively meal, complete with wonderful food and conversation—and lots of laughter. Darcy was beginning to realize how much these things had been missing from her life in New York.

"I hope you are all full and warm," Luke murmured softly after the main course, eyeing the double-decker chocolate cake Darcy had brought to the table. "Because after supper, I want to take you all for a sleigh ride."

Darcy stared at him. "A sleigh ride? I haven't been on one of those in years."

"Well, it's the perfect night for it. And there are a

bunch of us who are going to take the lumber trail up to the spruce grove. Maybe we can even pick out our Christmas tree while we're there.''

''Are we gonna have lights 'n everything?'' Jamie's huge blue eyes grew even bigger at Luke's nod. ''And an angel on top?''

''Oh, yes, we have to have an angel. It was an angel that brought the good news to Mary, remember?'' Clarice's voice was full of…what? Darcy asked herself. *Love and caring and happiness,* came the swift response as she watched that craggy face shine. And the funny thing was, she knew exactly how Clarice felt. She couldn't imagine her life without these people here to share in it. This Christmas *was* going to be special.

''All right, everybody in? Here we go then.'' Luke touched the reins and the horses set off down the road, their hooves clip-clopping at a steady, even gait.

''It's a perfect night, isn't it?'' Darcy tilted her head back to stare at the stars above. ''I can see the constellations as clearly as if the sky were a page in a textbook. Look, Jamie. There's the Big Dipper.''

Jamie leaned forward in his seat behind her and beside Clarice. ''We already found that, Mommy. An' I seed Cassy—what's it called again, Aunt Clarice?''

''Cassiopeia. And there's Orion's Belt.'' A lot of giggling and whispering ensued, and Darcy glanced at Luke.

''Thanks for thinking of this,'' she murmured. ''Jamie's thrilled and so am I. The sleigh bells are just the right touch, too.''

''Your dad got them. And made the sleigh, too—

at least part of it. I just finished it for him." He glanced sideways at her. "I'm sorry. I didn't mean to upset you."

"You didn't. I'm beginning to realize that a lot of what I remember was due to my mind-set. I let old hurts eat away at me until I'd manufactured them into something so monstrous that it took over my life."

"You mean, it wasn't as bad as you remembered?"

"To tell the truth, I don't know. Jalise asked me a while ago if there weren't some happy times here, and when I got started thinking about it, I realized that I'd only ever dwelt on the misery. I still don't remember a lot of good times, but every once in a while, a tickle of something happy twigs at my mind and I find myself smiling."

His gloved hand enfolded hers and squeezed. "I'm glad." He smiled, his breath a white foggy cloud around them. "You're too smart to let yourself be dragged down by the past."

"It's not all rosy," she warned, threading her fingers through his. "I still have days when I can't help asking why. Why didn't they love me? Why did they let me leave? But I'm beginning to realize that I may never know the answers to that. And I have to move on."

"I like the way you're moving on." His voice was low and feathered against her ear, his lips brushing her cheek. "You've done extremely well at school, I hear. The kids love you and even some of the teachers are singing your praises."

"It's just a matter of organization." But the warmth around her heart couldn't be denied.

"And you're a *master* at organization. The office

has never looked so good. It was a mercy you took it all in hand before Percy started asking for documents. I knew they were there but—''

''Where?'' she finished for him, laughing at his embarrassed look. ''It's actually not that difficult if you file something as soon as you're finished with it.''

''I'll try,'' he said in a humble, little-boy voice that made her giggle. ''How are your courses?''

''Well, I must confess, you were right. I was an idiot to take two at one time. Especially *those* two. But I love the psychology reading. It's fun. And English has always been a favorite of mine, although I must say I'm getting a little tired of Dickens. That's one paper I'll be happy to turn in.''

''Mommy, it's starting to snow!'' Jamie's excited voice cut through their conversation, his voice ringing with joy. ''Look, Mommy. Look!''

''I'm looking, sweetie.'' And Darcy was looking, a huge grin lifting her mouth. The whole world was like the inside of one of those glass snow domes that you shake to get the snow to whirl around. Fat white lacy flakes drifted down slowly, settling on the ground in a silent blanket of pure white.

''It's perfect,'' she whispered, catching one of the flakes on her tongue. ''Like a single frame of a memory that you have tucked away in your mind and pull out on special occasions to make you feel better.''

''It is nice, isn't it?'' Luke agreed as his arm wrapped around her shoulders. ''I'm awfully glad you're here to share it.''

''So am I.'' This was where she belonged. God had given her this one absolutely perfect night to help her understand that He was there, in control. Whatever happened, she could rest in His love and know that He would handle it all.

They glided on farther, and soon came upon other sleighs packed full of people traveling up the pretty path, fronds of overhanging evergreens shielding them from the snow.

"Let's sing," Clarice called from the back, and started off "It Came Upon A Midnight Clear." Seconds later the others joined in, their voices blending in an *a cappella* harmony that resounded through the valley.

"Why are we stopping?" Darcy whispered a few minutes later at the end of "Silent Night."

"There's going to be a campfire here. Someone came up earlier and cleared a sight. The Andersons brought hot chocolate, and I brought that pan of chocolate fudge you had cooling in the porch." His voice held a hint of laughter, but Darcy could see the question in his eyes.

"Good," she said, smiling when he squeezed her hand. "I want to contribute something, too." She pulled out the tin of shortbread she'd tucked under the seat and lifted the lid to show him. "We can set this out, too."

"It's not shortbread, is it?" He breathed, inhaling the buttery fragrance of the shapes. "I love shortbread!"

"My mother's special Scottish recipe. It'll melt in your mouth. Here, try one." Without a second thought, she popped the confection into his mouth and waited, her cheeks burning as his warm brown eyes rolled upward.

"Do we have to share that?" he teased in a whisper, his breath wafting across her ear. The faint motion sent a flurry of ripples up to her brain. "Maybe you and I could disappear into those woods with a thermos and this tin. No one would even notice." He jerked his head toward Jamie and Clarice who were already rushing toward the fire that glowed brightly in the darkness.

She followed his glance, her eyes noting that they were indeed alone. The others had abandoned their sleighs and were laughing and giggling round the fire.

"If I ask Clarice to watch Jamie, will you come for a walk with me, Darcy?"

She nodded, tucking a few cookies into her pocket, and the cookie tin back beneath the seat. A thrill of pleasure coursed through her. She couldn't believe she was with such a wonderful man.

He helped her down from the sleigh, placed a finger over her lips and, after tucking her arm through his, led her away from the others. Soon they were scurrying along a logging trail that Luke insisted, in a hushed whisper, he knew very well. Gradually, the voices of the others faded away until the forest closed around them, silent and waiting.

Which was exactly how Darcy felt. She didn't know what to expect next. Luke had always been warm and friendly with her. Lately he'd been more than friendly, and she'd welcomed the increasing warmth of their friendship. But tonight there was a special glow in his dark eyes that made her unexpectedly nervous. And happy. And excited.

"If we keep following this, we'll circle around the fire and eventually come back to where we left the sleigh. I came up here last year to get a Christmas tree for your parents, but we had tons of snow and I had to turn back. We ended up with a scrawny little spruce that I found over by the river." He smiled. "It didn't matter to your mother, though. She fiddled with it for days, and by Christmas Eve it was the most beautiful tree around."

"I'll bet she made little cinnamon gingerbread hearts and hung them on ribbons," added Darcy. "And potpourri sachets. She loved those. And mistletoe cookies. She used to make dozens of those to give away with the Christmas baskets that the church handed out."

"She didn't do a lot last year. She wasn't feeling all that spry. But she did manage to get something pretty special for those hampers. I asked her why she didn't just order something from the store and have it tucked in, and she said that it was important to—"

"—give something of yourself," Darcy finished. "She often said that. I remember a Christmas Eve when I went with her." Darcy stared up at the sky, remembering. "She used to disappear after the service, you know. Dad and I would stay at the church or go to the pastor's for a hot drink, and Mom would leave. She'd be gone about an hour and when she returned her whole face was lit up. I never could figure out what she was doing."

"I suppose you bugged her about it until she finally agreed to let you come along." Luke's tone was indulgent.

"Yes, she did. But only if I saved my allowance and got three gifts that I wanted but would give away.

It had to be something I really wanted for myself, you see. Otherwise she said it wasn't worth giving.''

"What did you get?"

"The first two were easy. Mason's in town had a huge bar of chocolate that I *really* wanted. I suppose you know that I like chocolate...."

"Like it?" Luke rolled his eyes, teasingly.

She grinned. "Anyway, I bought that. And they had a little sampler box with seven different perfumes in tiny little bottles that had gold tops. I'd coveted that for a solid month, and although there were only two left, I bought one of them. But it was the third gift that really caused problems."

"Because you didn't know what to get?"

"No, I knew what to get. But I didn't want to buy it just to give it away. Not at all—" she glanced up, feeling embarrassed "—greedy thing that I was."

"You could never be greedy," he murmured gallantly, his fingers tightening around hers. "What was this wonderful item?"

"You'll laugh," she warned, her cheeks growing warmer in the chilly air. Darcy stared at her boots. "It was a ten-piece manicure set."

"Files and stuff?" He frowned.

"A manicure set," she told him belligerently, wishing she'd never started this. "The kind of set that comes with all the trimmings including a bright red polish that I know I'd never be allowed to wear around the house. Everything a younger girl needs to look glamorous." With her eyes, she dared him to say a word.

"I see. So did you buy it?"

Butter wouldn't melt in that innocent, bland mouth,

Darcy noted. "Oh, I bought it all right. And a stuffed toy. I was going to keep the manicure set and give away the toy. I had everything wrapped and ready to go before the Christmas Eve service, and my mother called me into her room. She asked if I was certain that I was giving the three things that I most wanted for Christmas."

"And you told her?"

"I told her 'yes.' But before we left, I felt so guilty that I raced upstairs and exchanged the toy for that lovely set. It really hurt to wrap it up and carry it out to the car, and I spent the service praying that God would perform some miracle so that I wouldn't have to give it away."

Luke walked along beside her, her smaller hand nestled in his as they trod along the trail. Darcy was thankful for the silence as she organized her thoughts. He seemed to know that she needed the time and space to plunge on and finish the tale.

"After the service, my mother and I drove over to the east side. In those days it was a rundown area of Raven's Rest and a lot of people were suffering because the mill had closed down. She parked away from the houses, sort of in the dark, and took some things out of the trunk. I didn't know what they were, but I recognized some of the plates and tins as ones she'd frozen her baking in. There were gifts with name tags carefully spelled out on them and covered in bright foil paper with glittering bows. I could hardly believe it."

"Why?"

"Because I'd always been told not to waste money. My gifts usually came wrapped in newspaper or a piece of fabric with a hair ribbon on top. This was extravagance that I'd never seen before." Darcy swallowed past the strange lump in her throat, and continued.

"I followed her as she crept up to the doorstep and laid everything out on it. It took several trips at most of the houses, and I knew that was because there were so many people living in each. When we were all finished, she went back to the car. I was to knock on the door and then race away as quickly as possible. That part of it was fun."

She gulped down the tears that wouldn't stay out of her voice, and whispered so softly that no one else could possibly have heard. "They couldn't believe it. The parents turned on all the lights and everyone was so excited!" Darcy smiled. "I'll never forget those looks. I stayed hidden, you see. Disobedience again. But I wanted to know and so I hid in a bush or climbed up a tree. I remember the kids treated those gifts as if they were gold. They carried them so carefully, and I could see how stunned they were. It was amazing!"

"It must have been. It's a wonderful expression of Christmas spirit to pass on to a child." Luke's voice was full of meaning, and, for once, Darcy didn't take umbrage.

"Yes, it was."

Darcy could hardly bear to go on. "And I understood that what she was doing was important, believe me. I just couldn't accept that it wasn't right for me to have a little of that gold paper and ribbon that she lavished on everyone else. Now I wonder if perhaps there wasn't enough money to do both."

After a long silence, Luke's low voice broke the hush of the forest. "And the manicure set?"

"I was hoping you'd forget that," Darcy mumbled, keeping her face averted. "I left it at the last house we stopped at, and believe me, it was just about the hardest thing I'd ever had to do."

"Why? Surely you were resigned to giving it away by then?"

"Yes, but it was who it was going to. I knew who lived there, you see. Mary Pickens was the town's biggest gossip in those days. She spread a ton of rumors about me that I tried desperately to live up to. Her daughter, Annette, was my worst enemy at school, and she did every single thing she could to get me into trouble." She smiled bitterly. "Actually, not much has changed. She's still trying to get back at me through my job at the school now."

"And she's the one who got it?"

"Yes, Annette's the one who got my lovely Nail Galore kit. And showed her nails off every time I was around. She thought she was pretty hot stuff, and I would have liked nothing better than to tell her I'd given it to her because she and her mother were poor. Fortunately, I never let on. But the day she showed off her glamorous red nails, I was devastated. I'd dreamed about the difference it would make in my life, how beautiful I'd be. That kit had cost me every dime I had saved for weeks on end."

Luke wrapped an arm around her shoulders and hugged her against his chest, his genuine concern for her obvious. "I'm sorry you had such a hard time, Darcy."

She felt silly—but at least Luke seemed to understand how hard it had been to give the gift away.

"Yeah, so am I. But I guess it taught me a lot, too." Darcy searched for something to take the focus off her as she stood in the circle of his arms. "How about you? You must have some good memories of Christmases past."

He kept one arm strung round her shoulders as they resumed their walk. His voice was quiet in the waiting stillness.

"You mean with Macy? We only spent two of them together. The first one was at her parents'. We were engaged, but they didn't want her to marry me. It was not a happy occasion. By the second one we were expecting Leila, and Macy was feeling pretty rough. We were in California at the time, so we didn't even have snow. I suppose it wasn't the best of circumstances, but I didn't mind. I figured as long as we were together, everything was wonderful."

"She must have been very special." Darcy had gleaned a few details from Clarice—enough to know that Macy Lassiter had spunk enough to weather out the rough patches. She felt sad that Luke had lost his wife, but then, that loss had brought him here, to her. She couldn't, no, wouldn't be sorry about that.

"She wasn't perfect. Macy had her faults, but I loved her anyway. I couldn't believe it when they told me she'd died. And Leila, too. It was inconceivable to me that God would let such a thing happen."

"It does seem hard, doesn't it? Not to know why, and yet to have to accept it and go on." Darcy squeezed his fingers. "I'm sorry, Luke."

"I was, too. For a long time. That feeling sorry for

myself was what got me into trouble. I just sank deeper and deeper into my self-pitying world. Eventually I came to two conclusions.''

A silence stretched between them. ''Well, are you going to share them?'' Darcy prodded gently. ''It's only fair. After all, I've told you my personal stuff,'' she reminded.

''It isn't all that earthshaking. Or maybe it is. It's just that God is still God regardless of what happens. Nothing I can do or say will ever change that. He's always in control.''

''And the other conclusion?'' Darcy murmured, considering his words.

''The other is simply that I can either trust in that and follow His lead or I can trust in my own understanding and hope I scrape through somehow. When you get right down to it, it's not much of a choice, is it?''

''No, it's not much of a choice,'' she whispered, thinking of her own difficulty in accepting God's way.

''Anyway, I ended up here, working with your parents. They and Clarice helped me see that I'd been fortunate to have what I had. And they showed me that God was greater than my circumstance. I can't resent that. Besides, I met you and Jamie.'' He smiled down at her. ''Meeting you was quite an experience.''

''It was? Why?'' Darcy frowned, wondering if she should have asked. There were some things that it was better not to know.

''At first I thought you were just some spoiled brat. You know—a teenager that couldn't get along with her parents and ran away.''

"I was." Darcy grimaced at the truth of it.

"But there was more to the story. I've watched you face up to the townsfolks' small minds and grow from the challenge. You've raised a wonderful little boy who isn't afraid to explore things and, even better, has no idea that his life was full of hardships. Jamie treats problems like puzzles and that's due to you. Your love and nurturing have helped shape a child who will tackle life full-force. You're a very special woman, Darcy Simms, and I appreciate you more each day."

Luke stopped on the path, his hand on her elbow halting her amid the fresh pine-scented boughs. A hint of wood smoke reached them, but Darcy was oblivious to everything but the warm glow in those brown velvet eyes as Luke gazed at her. His head tilted down just a fraction, his lips mere inches from hers.

"I want to kiss you," he murmured, his mouth hovering above hers. "Is that okay with you?"

"More than okay," Darcy replied, raising herself on tiptoes as his lips slanted down over hers.

It was a soft kiss, a gentle, exploring kiss that asked questions and gave answers. Darcy couldn't help but respond to the thrill of it, her arms slowly moving around his neck as her fingers smoothed the silkiness of his dark nape.

When Luke buried his lips in her hair, Darcy leaned her head on his chest and breathed in the scent of horses and smoke and the fresh outdoors that lingered in his jacket. She linked her arms around his waist and stayed nestled in his arms, content.

"You're very special to me, Darcy," he whispered, tilting her head back so that he could see her eyes.

His thumb stroked her cheek. "I think I'm falling in love with you."

Darcy stared at him, unable to doubt the sincerity of his words. His eyes shone with joy and his lips were tender as they found hers once more. But what could she answer? She liked Luke; liked him a lot if the truth were told. And she enjoyed living on the ranch, watching him work with the animals, and share Jamie's little hugs.

Was that love? She'd thought she was in love once before, and it had turned to ashes in her hands.

How could she know?

"It's all right," he murmured, setting her carefully away from him. "You don't have to say anything. I apologize if I've offended you." He turned away to walk down the path.

Darcy caught up with him in several steps, amazed to see that they were now close to the campfire clearing.

"No, Luke. It's not that." She caught at his arm, forcing him to a halt. "I like you, too. Very much."

"But…?" He smiled sadly.

"But I'm not sure about the rest. Not yet." She sank onto a log. "I'm finding out things about my parents that I never suspected. And I'm learning things about *me* that are almost overwhelming. I never dreamed I'd be good at teaching—and yet I love it." She studied him, trying to gauge whether or not he understood her confusion.

"I feel like I'm uncovering a whole new me, sort of like digging for treasure and finding the contents of the chest aren't what you expected at all. And I like this new me. But I don't want to mess it up."

"And loving me would do that?" he asked.

"No, of course not. I just meant I don't want to blow it. Again." She drew in a deep breath. "I've made so many mistakes, Luke. I've done things wrong all through my life because I tend to rush into action before logically thinking things through. I don't want to rush anymore. I want to plan and take each step after I've carefully considered everything. No more rash behavior for Darcy Simms. Can you understand that?"

Luke sat down beside her, his legs thrust out in front. He was silent for several moments, his face inscrutable. Darcy shifted uneasily, wondering what he was thinking about, but deciding to let him sort through his thoughts in peace. When he did speak, she sat up straight, prepared for rejection.

"I guess it is all rather new," he agreed, turning to face her. "For you, anyway. I've known my own mind for a while now." He picked up her hand and enfolded it in his.

"I understand that you don't want to rush into anything. And I appreciate this new maturity you've gained. I think you never gave yourself enough credit before." He squeezed her fingers. "But, Darcy, I don't want to take any of that away. Love isn't about taking, it's about giving. I'm going to enjoy showing you that. So don't expect me to give up and go away. I won't. I'm here for the long haul. For you. Anytime you need me."

"Thank you," Darcy whispered, tears blurring her vision as she realized again what a wonderful man he was.

The only problem was her. Was Darcy Simms back in Raven's Rest permanently, or was this just another side road on her journey? And if it was, how could it include Luke Lassiter?

Chapter Twelve

When Darcy and Luke arrived back at the campfire, they met a very excited Jamie. The little boy told them that he and Clarice had invited a few people back to the ranch for some hot chocolate.

"Do you mind?" Luke stared at her intently, obviously gauging her reaction.

"No. No, I don't mind." The idea of visitors wasn't as repugnant as she would have thought.

Sleighs all followed Luke's, and soon the house was filled with guests. Christmas carols played on the stereo and the fireplace burned with a bright dancing flame as young and old milled around, sipping hot chocolate and punch that Clarice had hastily prepared.

"Haven't had folks over in a while. Thought it would be fun to have the place alive again." Clarice stopped suddenly and looked back at Darcy. "Should have asked," she muttered frowning.

"Of course you shouldn't! This is your home. And

a Christmas get-together is a great idea. Thank goodness we did the decorations yesterday,'' Darcy said.

"It's very kind of you to have us out here like this,'' Elroy Spiggot mumbled, and she turned to see him behind her, his eyes downcast. "'Specially with the things—''

Darcy cut him off, not wanting to hear about the past. This was the present and maybe, just maybe, her future. "Of course you're welcome, Mr. Spiggot. And you also, Mrs. Lancaster. Christmas is a time for friends and family, don't you think?''

Hilda Ridgely stood behind Ella Lancaster, a broad grin across her stern face. She winked at Darcy, and Darcy winked back, feeling happier than she had in years.

"Darcy? How are you?'' A tall, slightly graying man stood, hand outstretched, his smile quizzical.

"Jesse? Jesse Jones?'' Darcy noticed that René stood behind him. "Oh, no wonder René told me she's worried about you. You're old, Jesse!'' It was a timeworn taunt, and Jesse didn't let her down. He swung her up in a bear hug that threatened to crack her ribs, his laughter ringing out.

"If that isn't just like you, pip-squeak! Still so wet behind the ears, you don't know enough to respect your elders.''

"Not so wet, Jesse,'' Darcy murmured, watching as Jamie showed another child his train set.

"No.'' Jesse's voice dropped a bit, a hint of sadness running through it as he glanced at his wife. "I guess we've all aged a bit since those days.''

"Well, hopefully *some* of us have learned something.'' Darcy, striving to recapture the merriment, said to Jesse, "Wait till you see the costumes René's designed for the Christmas pageant. I'll bet you could market her patterns and retire from farming."

Given Jesse and René's history, it was the wrong thing to say—and Darcy knew it immediately. She waited for René to burst into tears or race from the room. She could already see the white lines radiating around Jesse's pinched lips. Surprisingly, René seemed deep in thought.

"I never thought of that," she murmured, her eyes far away. "The patterns and instructions are quite simple—even amateurs could assemble them. I could work out an assortment of themes—you know, English caroler, a Dickens' village."

"She's off!" Jesse grinned, but Darcy could see the relief in his eyes. "Now there'll be no rest for days while she ponders this."

"Do you good to stay up late once in a while." Luke playfully punched the other man in the arm. "You're getting staid in your old age."

"Staid? Ha! I can out-toss you in darts any day of the week, *old* buddy." They bickered playfully back and forth as they headed for the study, and Darcy knew they'd be engaged in a game shortly.

"It's a good idea though. Don't you think?" René asked. "I wonder if I couldn't work up something for a layette, too?"

Darcy stared at her. "A baby layette? Those are really hot right now. I've seen them in catalogs—the drapes, crib bumper pads, change table, quilt, pillows and a whole bunch of other things specifically designed to match. They cost a mint!"

René smiled, stroking her hand down her cheek.

"Exactly," she whispered, eyes shining. "And I could do it, Darcy. I could put together a package that would outshine anything that's out there right now." She grabbed the telephone pad and pencil, sank onto a kitchen stool, and began to jot things down. Darcy could only stare at the change in the unhappy woman's features.

Jalise entered the room and tapped Darcy on the arm. "Earth to Darcy! What's wrong with her?"

"She's decided to design a costume line and a layette line. I think." Darcy grinned. "Isn't it great?"

"It's great to see her so animated," Jalise agreed as she and Darcy moved into the hallway. "I just hope the layette idea takes root at home."

"What do you mean?"

"Jesse's wanted more kids for so long now, but René's always said Ginny's treatment had to come first."

"But Ginny does her exercises herself now," Darcy said. "You mean, it was just an excuse?"

"I think so. René always wanted lots of children. It's only since she came back that she's been so negative. And speaking of couples, what happened to you and Luke? You were both noticeably absent when I arrived at the campfire."

Darcy blushed. "We just went for a walk, Jay. Nothing unusual in that, is there?"

"That depends." Jalise's gray eyes narrowed. "What happened on this *walk* of yours? And spare me no details."

"We talked."

"And?"

"And Luke kissed me."

"Even better! And?"

"Do you have to know every detail?" Darcy glanced around, hoping everyone was busy with their own conversation. She had no desire to have this spread around.

"Yes, I do. Now tell me!"

"He said he loves me," Darcy whispered, a little in awe of the words herself.

"Finally." Jalise hugged her, enveloping Darcy in a cloud of flowery perfume. "It's about time."

"You mean...you knew?" Darcy felt as if her knees would give way. "How could you know?"

"It's perfectly obvious to anyone who's watched him watching you. He gets this calf-eyed look whenever he's with you. As if he's the proudest man in the world. What did you tell him?"

"That I needed more time. Well, I do," she insisted, ignoring Jalise's raised eyebrows. "I'm tired of messing up, Jay. If I'm going to settle down here, it has to be for the right reasons. I can't just use Luke as a way out. Do you understand?"

"Only because I know you and the convoluted way your mind works." Jalise's acerbic tones jolted Darcy. "You think you're not good enough or something silly like that, don't you."

"He's just lost his daughter and his wife. I've just lost my parents. We're both in a state of upheaval. We need time to sort through this, decide what we want."

"He's already said what he wants." Jalise tugged her into a corner, away from any potential eavesdroppers. "Macy and Leila have been dead for three years now. Luke's dealt with their loss. And now he wants to live again. With you. Isn't that what you want, too?''

"I like him, Jay. I like him a lot. He's so gentle and tender and yet he always knows exactly where he's going. And Jamie adores him.'' Darcy wrung her hands together. "But I was crazy about someone else once. And I made a terrible mistake. I'm a mother now. I can't afford to make another one."

"Another mistake like Josiah Pringle, you mean?" Jalise met Darcy's stare unabashed. "I guessed about him a long time ago, sweetie. But that's the past. And you are looking at the future. Aren't you?"

"Past, future—it all comes together eventually, Jay. Anyway, I'm going to turn it all over to God and let Him show me the way. And that means waiting on His timing, doesn't it?"

"Yes, I guess it does. I'm sorry, Dar. I didn't mean to push. It's just that I want you to be happy, and I think Luke would make you happier than you've ever been."

"Can I tell you a secret, Jay? I think he would, too."

I think he would, too.

A week later the words he had overheard still sent a tingle of joy to his brain. And Luke hugged the knowledge close to his heart. He hadn't blown it, hadn't overstepped himself. Darcy Simms did feel something for him. She just hadn't sorted it all out yet. But he intended to help her do it.

"You goin' to town again?" Clarice studied him as if he had a fever.

"Yes." He said it defiantly, to bolster his courage.

"I told Darcy I'd take her out after she finished her exam. It's near that time now. I thought maybe dinner at that Greek place that just opened. Can you manage Jamie?"

"Jamie and I been managing quite a lot lately. One more night won't hurt." Clarice stared at him. "You *mean* to wear one blue sock and one gray?"

Luke felt like an idiot as he scurried back up the stairs. Talk about acting like a teenager! Half an hour later he felt the same way as he sat outside the church waiting for Darcy. Pastor David had agreed to monitor her exam so she wouldn't have to go to Denver, and he knew that she was relieved not to have to travel. Thoughts of tonight occupied his mind for long moments after that.

Luke held his breath when she finally emerged. She looked okay, not as if she had been crying or anything. Wasn't that a good sign? He climbed out of the truck and walked the few steps to meet her, praying for the right words.

"Well?"

"I'm finished."

He rolled his eyes. "I know that. How did you do?"

She smiled at his angst. "Pretty well, I think. The questions weren't as difficult as I thought and I didn't skip one." She climbed in the truck, waited until he closed the door and came around to the other side. "I'm basically happy."

He frowned. "What aren't you saying?" he demanded after a moment, knowing something was hidden behind those deep, dark blue eyes.

She grinned a big happy grin that set her face

alight. "I think I did really, really well," she said finally. "I couldn't believe it. I just kept working my way down the page, thinking it's going to get worse. But it didn't."

"I knew you'd do it." He hugged her close, breathing in her scent as he did. "So now it's time for dinner on me. How about Stratos'?"

"I'm kind of keyed up. Do you think we could walk in the park for a little while? I need some exercise."

Luke shrugged. "I'm not really dressed for it," he told her sheepishly. "But I could use a little exercise myself." Especially since he seemed to be all thumbs at getting the key in the ignition. "Good thing they clear those walks for the joggers."

"I noticed you were all gussied up." Darcy's blue eyes teased mercilessly. "It's a good thing Jamie didn't see you. He'd be asking you all kinds of questions about that tie." She burst out laughing at his pained expression.

"It is a little loud, isn't it?" He laid one finger against the vivid tie. "Clarice gave it to me last Christmas and I don't want her to feel bad, so every once in a while I wear it."

"I think that's very nice of you. Most men would shove it in a drawer and try to forget it was there." She peered out the window as he drove through town. "Isn't it pretty? I love the way the lights sparkle on the snow."

"Christmas is special no matter where you spend it. But I guess it's always nicer at home." He let that sink in for a moment and then changed the subject. "I was talking to Jalise while I waited."

"How is she?" As soon as he pulled into the parking lot, Darcy was out of the truck and pulling in deep breaths of the chilly air.

Luke came around to her side and took her hand. Under the giant pines and huge spruce they walked, laughing together as a squirrel dashed across in front.

"Rooting for you. Also extremely curious. I had to answer a lot of nosey parker questions." He made a face to tell her how little he'd enjoyed the experience.

She giggled. "I can imagine."

"She wondered if you'd ever told me what made you leave Raven's Rest. You never have." He stared down into her eyes.

"Oh, Luke. I'm so happy, so excited. I don't want to ruin all that by dragging up the past again. This is a beautiful day, a wonderful season. Can't we just enjoy that?"

"Sure." He kept pace with her. "But when you want to talk, I'm here. I won't judge, I promise. We've all made mistakes, but those errors made us who we are today. And I really like who you are, Darcy Simms."

She smiled, a genuine, heartrending smile that made him forget everything but the fact that he was falling in love with this woman.

"You're so sweet, Luke. I know that I can trust you, that you wouldn't condemn. And I promise, I'll give you all the details. But not today, okay? Let's just enjoy this beauty." She whirled round and round in a circle, her arms embracing the world as her hair spun in a curtain of black.

"This is a perfect day. A wonderful, fantastic, deliciously perfect day." In a burst of ecstasy, she hugged him and then danced off down the path to return moments later with an icicle in her hands. "Look at this. Did you ever see such a big one? I knocked my two front teeth out when I was six trying to reach an icicle just like this."

He shivered, fully aware of just how insubstantial his dress clothes were for a walk in the park.

"I'm turning into one of those," he muttered to himself.

But Darcy heard him. Giggling, she tossed the icicle away, took his hand and hurried him back to the truck.

"You ranchers," she taunted. "You're such sissies. Us tough city girls outdo you every time."

He helped her into the truck and then switched it on, setting the heater to high. This teasing, laughing woman was such a change from the scared girl he'd first encountered, Luke couldn't help but join in the teasing.

"You city girls are full of hot air," he complained, backing out of the lot. "And you're no more a city girl than I am. Are you hungry yet?"

"Starved."

Ten minutes later they were seated at a table of a very nice Greek restaurant. After placing their orders, Luke began to tell Darcy about his youth.

Darcy giggled throughout the evening until Luke thought she'd burst. He knew she'd never imagined him as a bratty kid who got into everything.

"Didn't the teachers ever suspect that it was you who set the lab on fire with your experiment?" she asked. "Oh, these ribs are delicious!"

"Well, yes. Later. Actually, they were so excited

that I won the state competition, they didn't even reprimand me. I was Mr. Trip's pet student until the day I graduated." He regaled about his other antics while dessert was served.

"Brag, brag, brag." Darcy shook her head, pushing her plate away as she leaned back in her chair. "I am stuffed. Thank you, Luke. That was a wonderful meal. They certainly know how to cook here."

He nodded. "Yes, they do. And I like coming here because the booths give you a little more privacy than Jalise's café in town."

He'd no sooner uttered the words than an elderly couple stopped to speak to him about their horses. Moments later a neighbor followed, chatting about everything. He was followed by a group from the ladies' group who duly noted Luke's companion. They moved away, their whispers floating back.

"They're out together?"

"So much for a quiet dinner together," Luke said.

"It doesn't matter what they say," she whispered as he helped her away from the table. "We know that it was perfect."

Luke paid the bill, helped her don her coat and escorted her out of the restaurant. Outside, the sky was dark and bright with stars shining brightly overhead. They ambled across the parking lot to the truck.

"It's funny," she mused, staring up. "I don't think I ever even noticed the stars in New York. Here they're so bright."

"They sure are." But Luke was staring at the stars in her eyes. "Darcy," he murmured, his hands drawing her closer, "would you mind very much if those old girls happened to catch a glimpse of me kissing you?"

"They're gone," she whispered, holding his gaze with her own. "I saw them pull out a few minutes ago."

"Oh." He was disappointed with her answer.

"But, no, I wouldn't mind a bit. In fact I'd really like you to kiss me right now."

"Oh!" Luke saw the flicker of a smile waver across her lips and knew that she was as nervous as he. That made him feel a whole lot better.

He bent his head and kissed her, his lips touching hers, his breath melding with hers. As her arms slipped around his neck, Luke tugged her closer.

This was right. This was beautiful. This was what he wanted to last. He didn't need to know any more about her. He already knew everything that mattered.

He was deeply in love with Darcy Simms.

Darcy was walking on air. No, she was floating. Her exams had passed without a hitch and she felt certain she'd done well. School was out for the Christmas break, and life was wonderful. Of course, most of the reason for that feeling came from the man seated across from her, trying desperately to wrap his gift for Jamie.

"I detest gift wrapping," Luke muttered, tearing the pretty paper as he tugged his fingers away.

"Especially when you leave it till right before Christmas." Darcy giggled at the flecks of silver that had come off the paper and stuck to his nose where he'd scratched it. "Why didn't you ask for a box?"

"What kind of a box would fit this?" he demanded, glaring at the huge metal crane with a rotating arm that transported a bright yellow bucket on the end.

"Anything would be better than that. Why don't you hide it and put little scavenger-hunt notes under the tree? He'd love that."

Luke brightened at that idea. He wrapped the bulky item in a huge bath sheet and lugged it up to his room. Seconds later he was back with a pad and pencil, and busied himself scribbling.

"You shouldn't have spent so much on him, though. He's not used to it all." Darcy stifled thoughts of her own extravagance in the form of a shiny red-and-chrome bicycle she'd purchased, which now lay hidden in the barn. It was going to be the best Christmas Jamie had ever seen.

"And what do *you* want for Christmas?" Luke's hands tightened on her waist as he turned her into his arms with an ease that had become very familiar to Darcy. His mouth grazed hers in a light kiss.

"I have everything I want right here." Darcy ignored the niggle of conscience reminding her that she had one wish that wouldn't see the light of day—to know forgiveness. Instead she tightened her hands around his neck and kissed him back with abandon.

"Do you now? Well, then I might as well return your gift. It's pointless to try to improve on perfection."

Darcy giggled as his eyes danced with secrets. "Oh, you won't take it back," she assured him smugly.

"How do you know that?"

"You couldn't stand it. You can barely keep it a secret now." She kissed the tip of his nose and then wriggled out of his embrace. "Go do something, Luke, and leave me alone. I've got to get supper on. Clarice and Jamie will be back from their shopping trip soon, and we have that caroling party tonight."

"Are you sure you have warm enough clothes? It can get pretty chilly going door to door."

"Yes, I have some wonderful things, thanks to Clarice." Darcy smiled in reminiscence. "You know, that's one of the things that helped me decide to come back."

"Clothes?" He sounded amazed.

"Yes, clothes! You know very well that I had nothing nice and I didn't want to show up looking like a bum. Clarice's wonderful gift gave me a sense of dignity that I hadn't felt in a long time. It was as if I could hold my head up again because someone cared about me enough to think of that small detail."

Darcy turned on the oven and slipped a casserole inside. "Clarice is the most perceptive woman I know. She manages to make you feel needed and wanted without emphasizing how much you need her. I think it's a special gift. I only hope I can pay her back someday."

"She's happier than I've ever seen her, and that's due to you," Luke told her. "You have a knack for helping people find themselves."

"Rather strange, don't you think? Especially since it's taking *me* so long to find myself." Darcy rinsed off her salad ingredients. When Luke's hands closed over her shoulders, she jumped in surprise, but allowed him to turn her to face him.

"You're finding yourself right on God's schedule," he murmured. "And you've touched lives along the way. René Jones is thrilled about the idea you gave her. I talked to Jesse yesterday and he said it's as if she has a new lease on life."

Darcy blushed, but the warm glow that spread through her body wasn't entirely due to Luke's presence. For the first time in a very long while she felt proud of what she was doing.

"Well, if I helped, I'm glad. I like René. Speaking of which, I have to get the last bit of braid sewn on that costume. I'm going to take it and that baking into town when we go tonight."

Luke stopped munching on his carrot. His eyes narrowed. "You're not giving away the shortbread, are you? I never did get to taste that—"

"As I recall, I offered you some—" Darcy set the table, hoping he would ignore her red face "—but you were too busy."

"Yes, I was. Too busy falling in love with you." His lips brushed the top of her head. "You're quite a woman, Darcy Simms."

"I'm glad you think so." She slipped out of his arms and sank onto a nearby chair to tack the thick gold braid onto the wise man's costume. She drew a sigh of relief as Luke went whistling out the door, and let the fabric fall to her lap.

Chapter Thirteen

"The caroling was fun, wasn't it?" Luke tucked her hand into his and held on as he negotiated the highway drive home.

In order for him to hold her hand, Darcy had to move closer. Which wasn't a hardship, she decided happily.

"It was lovely. The seniors in the apartment complex were so excited to have someone come and sing to them. It must be lonely." She thought about her parents together on the farm, and was glad that they had had each other.

Luke turned the truck into the yard. Darcy escaped out of the truck before he could catch her and raced across the yard laughing, almost making it up the stairs before his fingers caught hers.

"Hey, don't I get a good-night kiss?" he demanded, his arms going about her waist.

"You sure have a lot of reasons why I should kiss you." Darcy considered them all. "There's the good-morning kiss, the breakfast kiss, the kiss at coffee time, the just-because kiss, the dessert kiss after lunch, the help-me-make-it-through-the-day kiss, pre- and post-dinner kisses…''

"But this has to be the best one of them all," he whispered as his mouth neared hers.

Darcy held her breath, waiting, but when he didn't kiss her, she asked the question that lay uppermost in her mind. "Why?"

"Because this one has to last me until tomorrow morning." And then he gave her the most tender kiss. "I love you, Darcy," he murmured at last, his lips buried in her hair.

Darcy couldn't hold in her response. It surged up from the depths of her heart and she could no more have stifled it than stopped breathing.

"I love you, too, Luke. Very much."

He pushed away gently to peer down into her eyes. "You do? Really? I mean—I always knew you would someday, but I just didn't expect—that is, I thought you needed time, and I was going to give it to you—"

"Lucas?" Darcy interrupted.

"Yes?"

"Do you think you could stop talking and kiss me again? After all, it is a very long time until my good-morning kiss."

And Luke proceeded to do as he was told.

"I'm going home!" René Jones clapped a hand to her head. "Everything that can go wrong is going wrong with this Christmas pageant. I knew it would."

Jalise seemed to be of the same opinion. "It was just too grandiose. We should have known that."

Darcy glared at both of them. "Jalise Penner, don't you dare cop out on me now. I need you to go and get what's left of those Christmas pageant props into place. René, if you're going to be sick, go to the bathroom. Has anyone seen Luke?"

"I'm sorry, Darcy. I haven't felt well for days. It's usually just in the mornings, though. I'm always fine by this time of the day." René's greenish-white face had Darcy searching for Luke. "I don't know what's wrong with me lately."

"I do." Darcy glanced from one to the other of her friends. "Oh, brother! You two were the science brains. Don't you know anything about pregnancy?"

"Pregnant? René?" Jalise gaped.

"Pregnant? Me? But I wasn't even trying!" René abruptly sat down, her face losing what little color it had.

"Yes, well, trust me. Sometimes it happens that way." Darcy was amazed that she could joke about the past this way. But then again, someone had to do something. The whole play was going to flop if they didn't!

She called to Luke, who was on the other side of the stage. "Find Jesse, will you? René needs him." When Luke didn't move, Darcy went over to him and whispered in his ear. His face wreathed in smiles, Luke returned moments later with a stunned Jesse.

"René? Are you sure?" The tender look on the big man's face brought tears to Darcy's eyes. How could René doubt that this man loved her?

"No, I'm not sure. Not at all." René patted Jesse's cheek. "But Darcy is."

"I pray that it's true," he said in wonder.

"Well, for now you're going to have to assume it is, and get her out of here. Go find a seat in the audience if you must hang around. We've got a show to put on." Darcy squealed when Jesse enveloped her in a bear hug. "Jesse, it's ten minutes till show time! Get out of here."

"Oh, it's so wonderful!" Jalise wept as she watched Jesse usher his wife from the crowded and rather hot stage.

"Jalise, get hold of yourself! We've got to get these children lined up. Now, the choir goes out front first, right? Luke, you make sure they've all got their bows and cummerbunds on. Then line them up in the hall. There should be thirty-two of them." She squeezed his hand and let him go. "What comes first, Jay?"

Somehow they had everyone in their place by seven, and the curtain went up on time. Cheery little voices carried the timeless hymns off without a hitch, and even "Joseph," who'd been sick ten minutes before, played his part regally.

"It was a wonderful evening!" Ella Lancaster shook Darcy's hand after the performance. "Just wonderful."

Darcy finally had to pull away to nab one of the wise men, and get him to remove his shimmering velvet robe. But she deliberately remained behind the curtain to allow Jalise and René their moment in the sun.

"Tired?" Luke helped her hang up the costumes and fold away the last of the bright red cummerbunds. "It's okay if you are. You've earned it."

"Mommy, I liked your show." Jamie stood suck-

ing on a candy cane beside Clarice's tall, spare form.
"Did you like our class song?"

"Thank you, darling. And I loved your song."
Darcy hugged him tightly. "I need to stay here and
clean up. Would it be all right if I imposed once more,
Clarice?"

"Not an imposition! I love Jamie. We'll go home
and sit in front of the fire, and I'll read him the Christmas story. When you come home, you can tuck him
in."

"Thank you, Clarice." Darcy hugged the older
woman with a heart full of love. "You are very special to both of us."

Seconds later Darcy and Luke were alone, packing
away the items to leave the platform free for the next
day's service.

"I thought if I got it all put away tonight, I could
have Christmas and the following day off without stirring from the house. I'm worn out."

"You look pretty good to me," Luke said, taking
her in his arms.

Reluctantly, several moments later, Darcy pulled
herself away to finish her work. "That's it! Let's go
home."

Luke silently helped her on with her coat and
waited as she switched out all the lights. At the truck
he held open the door and Darcy climbed in.

"I like the sound of that," he murmured as he
climbed in the driver's side, letting the engine idle
while he studied her.

"The sound of what?" Darcy could barely lift her
eyelids.

"Home. A real home. For you and me. And Jamie. And Clarice, too, if she wants."

Darcy's eyes did fly open at that. She stared at him.

"I'm talking about the future, Darcy. Our future. Together. Will you marry me?" Luke didn't wait for her answer. "You said you loved me. And I love you more than I could ever tell. There was pain in each of our lives until God brought us here together. I'm glad He did because I want to marry you. I want us to be a family. I don't care about the ranch. It's yours to do with as you see fit. We can go anywhere you want. All I ask is that we go together."

Wild unbridled joy brought tears to her eyes as she stared into that dearly beloved face.

"Darcy? Is it too soon?" Luke's voice was hesitant. "I'll understand if you need more time. Maybe you need to think it through more clearly. I know you wanted to be sure you are doing God's will. Maybe—"

"Luke?" Darcy waited until his dark fathomless eyes focused on her. Then she whispered her answer. "Yes."

He seemed stunned. "You mean it? Really? But I thought—no, never mind all of that. Yes?"

He wrapped his arms around her and kissed her, his heart filled with joy. And then, while Darcy sat beside him, he drove home singing "Joy To The World" in the flattest, most off-key voice she'd ever heard. But it sounded beautiful to her ears.

Darcy was amazed at his ability to get Jamie into bed without a protest. And she watched, amused, as Clarice huffed off to her room after an unsubtle hint from her nephew. But Darcy wasn't prepared for the small black velvet box he handed her as they sat before the fire.

"Merry Christmas, Darcy. With all my love."

She caught her breath at the beautiful solitaire diamond perched high on the thick gold band. And she still wasn't sure that she was breathing when he slipped it onto her finger.

"When can we get married?" he demanded. "When can we tell Jamie? Will he mind? How about giving him a wonderful Christmas and then telling him after things quiet down. Then we can reassure him how much we both love him." Darcy started laughing as tears flooded her face. "Darcy? Oh, my. Here, mop up, darling. I'm sorry."

He held her close, and soon Darcy did stop crying. But she couldn't stop the smile that spread across her face. "I love you, Luke Lassiter. And every day I thank God that He sent you to bring me back here." She kissed him, returning his love with her own.

Luke leaned back against the sofa, Darcy cradled in his arms as he stared into the fire.

"What are you thinking about?"

His eyes glowed in the firelight and he traced one finger down her cheek to her mouth.

"I was just wondering if that was my good-night kiss, a thank-you kiss or an I-love-you kiss. I do like to keep them all straight." His mouth quirked in a tiny grin.

"That was a just-because kiss," Darcy informed him, rising to her feet as she lifted Jamie's stocking down from the mantel. "And if you help me get these filled, I'll show you my good-night kiss. That way you won't get mixed up again."

Luke complied with a swiftness that had her giggling uncontrollably when she finally went to bed. She held her hand up in the shaft of moonlight shining through the window and admired her ring for the umpteenth time, even though a big wad of tape kept it securely on her finger. They'd have it sized and then, after New Year's, they'd tell the world their news. Meanwhile, it was their special secret and she would hug it to herself.

Thank you, Lord. Thank you very much for Luke Lassiter. I'll try to get it right this time. I'll try not to make any mistakes. But if I do, could you please forgive me? I'm not very good at this loving thing yet. But I will be, she promised. *I will be.*

It was the most wonderful Christmas Darcy could ever remember. Fresh snow left the sunny world outside glistening and gleaming with a brightness that almost hurt her eyes.

Jamie was ecstatic over his bicycle and insisted on riding it once around the living room, much to Darcy's dismay. At least the training wheels prevented any falls.

Clarice seemed delighted by the bright teal-and-royal-blue angora shawl that Darcy had crocheted. "I've never had anything so lovely," she murmured, brushing her knobby fingers across the gossamer softness. "It's perfect."

"It's nothing compared to the wardrobe you gave me when you didn't even know me." But Darcy accepted her hug. "And I love these dishes. I didn't know you could fire so high and still get such a bright glaze. I'm going to enjoy using them. And Jamie's wooden spoons will be perfect for stirring.'' She knew her son had earned the money helping Luke, and she let her eyes express her thanks to him.

But it was Luke's face that she focused on and Luke's smile she waited for as he opened the last gift under the tree. As he pulled out the rust-colored cardigan she'd made, Darcy felt a glow of satisfaction. She'd thought to buy him something as a gift, but this was straight from her heart, and, somehow, she thought he would appreciate it the most.

He caught her under the mistletoe later that day to tell her how much he appreciated the labor of love. ''I'll wear it often. It'll feel like your arms around me,'' he whispered, just as his lips covered hers.

They enjoyed a relaxed fun day which included a sleigh ride through one of the meadows. And when they took a few minutes to renew their pledges of love, Jamie and Clarice didn't seem to mind. The turkey, plump and golden and dripping with succulent juices, sat in the middle of the table. And as they joined hands around it and bowed in prayer, Darcy couldn't help glancing around at the ones she now called family. She echoed Luke's words.

''Father, you've blessed us abundantly. Not just with physical gifts, but with each other. Most of all You gave us Your son to show us the way to You. Bless us now and keep us ever mindful of your great sacrifice. Amen.''

''Amen,'' Jamie added, beaming from ear to ear.

Chapter Fourteen

Darcy glanced at the roomful of six rowdy children and blew her bangs from her forehead. Maybe having such a large birthday for Jamie after the Christmas rush hadn't been such a good idea. She'd planned a sledding party but worried that it was too cold.

"Get 'em outside in that air and let 'em run," Clarice advised dourly. "January's a good month to get fresh air."

"And it *is* fresh!" Darcy glanced at the thermometer and shivered. "You don't think it would be too cold for them?"

"Not likely! These are hardy children and they're dressed for the weather. Let them go sledding for a while and see if that doesn't tire them out."

"Okay, kids. We're going sledding. Get your snow pants and jackets on." With Clarice's help, Darcy got them dressed, one by one, and outside. Jamie led the way to the ridge behind the house that provided the perfect incline for a toboggan ride.

"Now listen to me. We have to go on this side. Nobody is to go over there. It's really dangerous because of the trees."

She shepherded them to the left, and watched as Jamie hurtled himself down on the racer Clarice had given him. In a matter of moments he was at the bottom, and Darcy let out her pent-up breath in relief.

Down they went, some on plastic sheets, some on sleds or toboggans and some on the seats of their pants. Their hilarity was a joy to behold, and Darcy grinned as she watched Jamie land upside down in a soft puffy snowbank.

"Looks like a pretty good time," Luke murmured as he came up behind her, his arm sneaking around her waist. "Want to try it?"

"Me?" Darcy stared at him. "I'm a little too big, don't you think?"

"No, I don't. Nobody is ever too old to go sliding. Come on." And before she knew it, Darcy was seated behind him, flying down the hill on a flat piece of waxy cardboard. They fell off near the bottom, much to the amusement of the kids, and Darcy couldn't help but laugh as she dusted herself off.

"Now comes the hard part, old girl. We have to climb all the way up that hill," Luke said with a laugh.

"Hey! Who are you calling *old?*" And Darcy raced up the face of it just to prove that she could, gasping and wheezing when she finally reached the top.

The group of six whooped and hollered their way back to the house and descended on the table like a herd of locusts. Clarice kept them in line until Darcy could light the cake and supervise the singing. And Luke stood ready with a camera, snapping pictures wildly as Jamie blew out all five candles. Watching the happy kids gulp down cake and juice, Darcy leaned back against Luke, relishing the feel of his arms around her.

"It's hard to believe he was born five years ago. He's so grown up. I wish my parents had met him, held him. I was so stupid to go running off. But I couldn't think of any other way." She roused herself, determined not to cling to the past. "At least he's healthy and happy. Thanks to you and Clarice."

"And you." Luke's eyes darkened. "You're a wonderful mother, Darcy."

"Thank you."

"How long till we take these guys home?"

"I promised they could watch the rest of that video. About twenty minutes more," she vowed. "Then the bedlam will be over."

Twenty minutes almost to the second, Luke returned to watch as the tape ended and then called for the group to get their coats.

"Can I help take them home, Mommy?" Jamie asked.

"I don't think so, sweetie. There wouldn't be enough seatbelts for everyone. You could help me clean up, though."

But once the other children had left, Jamie wasn't inclined to be helpful. He wandered here and there, unable to settle to anything. When Clarice offered to play a game, he snapped at her, and Darcy was forced to send him to his bedroom.

"When you can speak politely, you can come out.

Birthday or no birthday, we remember our manners, son.'' He blinked up at her tearfully, his mouth tipped down, and Darcy felt her heart contract with love.

"Why don't I have a daddy, Mommy? The other kids all do. But I never had one. Not even one. Jimmy Wiggins has two!''

Darcy sucked in her breath. How could she ever tell Jamie about his father? Whatever happened, she wanted to shield him from the truth.

"We talked about this before, son. Remember? Some children don't have a daddy. But that's okay. Because we have a Father in heaven that loves us very much.''

"It is *not* okay!'' He glared at her. "It's not fair. I want a daddy to do things with. I want my own daddy so he can tuck me in at night, an' play baseball an' lots of stuff.'' His voice had become shrill. "Why can't God get me a daddy, Mommy? Doesn't He love me enough?'' Jamie was sobbing loudly, his little body stiff and unyielding as she tried to hug him.

"Honey, I need to tell you…'' Darcy prayed for some heavenly help, searching her mind for answers. Maybe she could tell Jamie that she and Luke…but no. Luke wanted to do that when they went out for dinner. It would be his very special birthday gift. "Jamie, there's something—''

"No!'' Jamie jerked away from her restraining hand and threw himself across the bed.

Unable to reason with her son, and knowing that he was tired from all the excitement, Darcy ignored the outburst, brushing his forehead with a kiss before she went back downstairs.

"Everything all right?" Clarice had the table cleaned off and the dishes half washed.

"Yes, he's just tired. He asked me about his father."

"And?"

"What could I say?"

"You could have told him that Luke would be his new father," Clarice said. "You could have told the whole town when you told me."

"I would have, but Luke wanted to tell Jamie first, once the Christmas rush and the excitement of his birthday were over. We were planning on doing it tonight. Oh, well. He'll sleep a bit and be back to his cheerful self."

But when Darcy went to get her son for supper, his bed was empty. She searched every room, scoured every closet and hunted under every bed to no avail. Jamie was nowhere to be found!

"Where could he be, Clarice?" A shaft of fear shot through her heart as she noticed the empty hook by the door. "His coat is gone!"

"Probably went out to the barn," Clarice guessed. "He loves to sit with those animals."

Darcy raced back into the house seconds later, breathless from her search. "I called and called and he didn't answer. Where *is* he, Clarice?"

"I don't know." The older woman paled visibly. *Lord, we need Your help and we need it now.* She looked up as Luke drove into the yard. "I'll get my coat on. You go get Luke to help you start looking outside. I'll check all around in here one more time."

Luke insisted on searching the barns, workshop and garage, and, unable to think of another solution,

Darcy tagged along. But it was dark in each building, and outside the wind had stiffened, icy particles stung their cheeks.

"I don't know, sweetheart. I just can't understand where he'd go. But we'll find him, don't worry. Thankfully, they finished sledding before this sleet hit. The hill would be sheer ice by now."

Darcy stopped in her tracks, grunting when Luke careened into her. "Luke—the sled! Do you think he would have gone sledding by himself?"

"Let's see if it's missing."

It was.

"Call him and keep calling," Luke ordered. "I'm going to get the truck and a rope. If it's as icy as I think, we'll need something to hang onto. Besides, the truck lights will help. Meet me at the hill."

"Jamie! Ja-mie!" She called, but the wind tore the words away before she'd reached the hill and peered down into the little valley below. Darcy screamed it out again and again, but no answer came.

Luke drove up behind her in the truck. "Okay, Darcy, I've got a rope on and I'm going down. You stay here."

"I'm not staying here! That's *my* son we're looking for."

"I might need help to get him up. If I tell you, you can come down, but put a rope on first. There's one on the seat." He kissed her hard and then rappeled over the edge, his boots clacking on the ice.

Darcy watched as he moved through the headlights. *Please God, don't let Jamie die. He's just a child, an innocent little boy. Don't make him pay for my sin. He's been such a joy to me, such a gift when I needed someone special. And he loves it here. Please God, don't let him be hurt.*

She continued to pray even while fearing that it was doing no good. Every so often she paused to call out her son's name, but there was no answer. Clarice came out shortly after, her face grim.

"I've searched every nook and cranny. He's not inside."

"Darcy, I've found him!" Luke's voice came faintly up the hillside. "He's been injured."

Darcy swayed at the words, her heart in her throat. *Lord, this mother and son need Your mighty touch right now,* Clarice prayed. *Stay near, Heavenly Father and keep that child safe in Your hands.* Clarice hugged Darcy close. "He'll be all right," she promised. But there was a starkness to her voice that Darcy recognized as fear.

"Darcy? I need another rope. Tie it onto the front and then toss it down. Make sure it's tied tight. Get Clarice to help you."

"I'm here, boy." Clarice moved with purpose, urging Darcy out of the way as she found the coil of rope and fixed it firmly to the front of Luke's half-ton. "Always hated trucks. Changing my mind tonight." She grunted with the effort of tossing the rope over the edge, then walked back and climbed into the cab.

"Did you get it?" Darcy was unaware of the cold or the wind except as they would interfere with the rescue of her son. "Can you get him up?"

"No. He's unconscious, I think. And it's too slippery for me to climb back up. I'm going to tie him to the sled. When I give the word, tell Clarice to back up very slowly. I'll try to get a foothold as we go. Got it?''

"Yes, we've got it.'' Darcy nodded at Clarice.

Why should her child have to pay for all the stupid, senseless mistakes she'd made? Why hadn't she told him about Luke when she'd had the chance? Why was God letting this happen?

New knowledge seeped into her brain slowly. God didn't want her to marry Luke! She wasn't worthy. This was His judgment on her for the many times she'd rejected Him and scorned to follow in the path He'd directed. It was a lesson, that's what it was. A lesson in what might have been if she hadn't ruined it all with her stupidity.

It was pure agony to wait for Luke's return up the hill. With every creak of the truck, Darcy shook in fear, berating herself for her folly. Pleading and promising, the words rolled toward heaven mindlessly, each one begging for mercy for Jamie. But God's mercy seemed a long way off as she caught sight of Luke and her son moving into the truck's glare.

Jamie lay still and white on the sled, his head tilted to one side. She sucked in her breath at the huge, purplish lump on his forehead. With dread dragging at her conscious mind, Darcy knelt and brushed his hair back.

"Honey, it's Mommy. Can you hear me? I was so afraid. You weren't supposed to slide near the trees, son. It's too dangerous. Jamie? Please wake up.''

"Come on, Darcy. We've got to get him to the hospital. I don't know what other injuries he may have.'' Luke was trying to undo the ropes that held the little boy to the sled, but his fingers were cold and clumsy. Clarice brushed them away and undid the knots with her bare hands, her voice soft.

"It's all right, Jamie. Auntie Clarice is here. I'll help you. And so will Uncle Luke. And your mommy. You don't have to be afraid. We're not mad." But even for his beloved Clarice, Jamie would not wake up.

Darcy's black curtain of despair would not be lifted, not when they reached the hospital, not when the attendants lifted Jamie onto the stretcher, not when the doctors shut her out of his room, and not when Luke's arms wrapped around her.

"He's in God's hands, sweetheart. And God loves little children. Jamie's going to be fine."

She jerked away, and Luke let her go, his arms falling to his sides. He watched as she walked over to the window and peered mindlessly out at the falling snow. "He'll be fine, darling."

But Darcy wouldn't listen, wouldn't allow herself to be consoled. She knew the truth. God was a just God, a fair God. He couldn't let a sinner like her get away with all her misdeeds just because she was sorry for them. How many times had her parents told her that every sin had a price?

She watched as an ambulance pulled up to the entrance, her mind grappling with the situation.

"All right," she whispered brokenly. "I'll do whatever it takes to keep Jamie alive."

Including leaving Luke and Clarice? Leave this place, turn your back on everything? Darcy could hear the question reverberate through her mind and she turned to glance at the man she had come to love so deeply. *Will you give up everything you've found, as a punishment for the wrong you've done? Will you leave here and never return?*

The very thought of it made her gasp with agony, but Darcy resolutely turned away from Luke's frowning face and stared out into the blackness.

Just let Jamie be all right, God, she murmured. *I'll leave here right after that. I'll go back to New York. I'll manage whatever You send. Just let him live.*

As if in direct response to her tearful plea, the doctor walked into the waiting room, his eyes darting from Luke to her. "Miss Simms?"

"Is he all right? Is Jamie going to be okay?" Darcy sent up one last prayer.

"I think so. We're reasonably certain that your son has suffered a concussion, but since there is some swelling at the back of the head, we'll have to wait until he wakes up. The sooner he does that, the better I'll feel." He smiled encouragingly. "In the meantime, I've ordered some tests, just to be certain."

"Can I see him?" Darcy started for the door.

"Miss Simms, we've moved him into 108. I, er, that is, don't be too concerned about the equipment you'll see in there. We're monitoring everything, just to be sure. Also, he has a broken arm." She nodded and stepped past him, hurrying down the hall to her son's room, her heart filled with joy. A broken arm— what did that matter? It would heal. As long as he was all right....

But how could she do it: tear herself away from everything that had become so precious in these past few months? How could she just leave, as if nothing mattered? As if she wouldn't leave behind a piece of her heart with the big, lanky rancher who'd come to mean so much to her?

"I can deal with it," she kept telling herself as she walked. "As long as Jamie is okay, I'll handle the rest, no matter what."

Jamie lay on the narrow bed, his body covered by a sheet. The lump on his forehead was blossoming with color, but his eyes were closed. Darcy noted the rhythm of his chest, assuring herself that he was still breathing.

Thank you, God. She inhaled, her fingers closing around his still ones where they stuck out below the edge of the cast. *Thank you for looking after my son.*

Tears welled as she listened to the steady *beep* of the heart monitor. Near his head, a machine scribbled a wild variation of lines on a continuous piece of paper. *Oh, dear Lord, please let it be okay.*

"Mommy's here, Love Bug. Right here beside you. You're all right. I won't let anything hurt you." She pressed a butterfly-soft kiss against his cheek, sucking in a tortured breath when he didn't respond.

"Darcy? Don't cry, honey. He's going to be all right! The doctors think he'll wake up pretty soon now." Luke turned her in his arms and let her bawl, his hands gently soothing on her back.

And for several long moments, Darcy let him, storing up the memory for the future. It was all she would have to remember of him. Then she tugged herself away, dashing the tears from her cheeks.

"He'll get better by leaps and bounds when he finds out we're getting married, Darcy! I just know—"

"We're not getting married, Luke," she said, ignoring the stab of pain the words brought.

"Sure we are. We'll have to wait till he's better, of course. But that won't be long. And then we'll be one big happy family."

"No, Luke." She shook her head adamantly, fingers closing in a fist of determination. "I'm sorry, but I can't marry you."

"What?" He frowned, staring at her. "Why?"

"Because this isn't the place for me. It never has been." She used the old argument, knowing that he wouldn't try to compete against what he thought of as the bright lights of the big city. "I can't live in a one-horse rinky-dink town for the rest of my life. There are places I need to go, and things I want to do before I die."

"And you're just figuring that out now?" His face was a mask of self-control. "After all this time, you've suddenly forgotten exactly what your life in New York was like?"

"No." She couldn't meet his gaze and so she turned and focused on her son. "But that's not going to happen again. I have some references now. I can work in a school during the day and finish my studies at night. Besides, I'll have my half of the money from the ranch. You can buy me out. Jamie and I'll be fine."

"And it doesn't mean anything to you—leaving the heritage your parents gave to you?" His tone was sour. "What about Jamie? What about your son's future? Doesn't he deserve a life of security?"

"I'm doing this for him," she whispered brokenly. "So that he doesn't get driven to the same lengths I

was, so he doesn't have to make the same mistakes."
She swallowed. "And I'm doing it for you, too, Luke.
You have no idea of the things I've done, the mistakes I've made. If you did, you wouldn't want to
have anything to do with me. You should be glad I'm
sparing you the pain. I'm doing it to help you."

"No, you're not." Luke laughed bitterly, the sound
harsh in the quiet room. "You're leaving because
you're running scared. Why not admit it? You can't,
or won't, let yourself trust in God and wait to see
what's in the future for us. *You've* got to be in control,
Master Planner Darcy Simms!"

His scorn chipped away at her hard-won control.

"You don't understand," she croaked.

"Sure I do. I love you and Jamie both. I thought
you loved me—that you and I would make up for the
pain of the past. But at the first hint of trouble, you
bolt, just like you've always done." His eyes hardened. "You say you loved your parents, but I'm beginning to wonder about that. Love doesn't stick its
tail between its legs and run scared when the going
gets tough, Darcy. Love endures."

"I do love you, Luke. But I'm leaving out of love,
too. Please don't be angry. I just have to go."

"No, you don't have to!" He strode across to the
door and yanked it open. "That's the saddest thing
about it. You could have waited until Jamie woke up.
We could have told him what we'd planned and he
would have been ecstatic. But you won't wait and see
what happens. You might get hurt or things might
turn out differently than you think."

He sighed, lowering his voice. "When will you
learn to trust, Darcy? To trust me? To trust God? To

trust that the whole world isn't out to get you before you get them?'' He studied her face sadly. ''Our future could have been something great, you know. It still can be. Please, just think things out a little more clearly. Pray about it.''

''I have prayed, Luke. Long and hard. And I've never been as sure as I am right now that I made the right decision.'' She stared down at Jamie's dark head on the white pillow. ''As soon as the doctors say he's able to travel, we'll be leaving Raven's Rest.''

Chapter Fifteen

That Jamie was well and had been released from the hospital was wonderful. But with it came the knowledge that Luke's precious Darcy would be leaving. Before she did, Luke had to tell her something important.

Please God, show me the right way to do this.

"Darcy, can I talk to you?" he said after dinner the next night. She glanced at him warily. "In the office would be the best. I have something I need to give to you."

He was relieved when she said nothing, but simply followed him into the perfectly organized room. Dully, he wondered how long it would be before everything was a mess again.

"Yes?"

"Darcy, I know I should have given these to you long ago. Your parents asked me to make sure you got them. I was saving them for a special occasion, but I guess this is the best time." He removed the brown envelope from the filing cabinet and held it out. "Your mother left this in my care, to give to you when you came home."

She took it, her fingers careful to avoid his. He saw the way her face blanched as she stared down at the familiar writing, and he felt the pain all the way through his heart.

"I'll leave you alone to read them. Jamie's watching the television. I'll stay with him."

Darcy nodded, then slit the envelope and slipped out the pages covered in her mother's perfect script.

My dearest Darcy,
For so long we've searched for you, longing for the day when you would come home and be with us again. Now it looks like we're not going to find you in time. So I'm writing this as our apology. Dad and I know we made many mistakes raising you. But dearest girl, we just wanted the best for you. And we thought that if we were very strict and instilled a sense of responsibility in you, you would rise to the wonderful life God had planned for you. In our concern to do everything by the book, we forgot the most important part of parenting—love.

Darcy stared, unable to believe what she was reading. Could it possibly be true? Were Clarice and Luke and even Jalise right when they said that Martha and Lester had loved her?

These past five years, I've wondered so many times if things would have been different if we'd told you from the beginning that you were adopted. Would it have explained anything to know that my youngest sister, Dora, got pregnant with you by a man who hadn't told her he had a wife and a family? Would you have understood how badly we wanted to keep the stigma from you by ensuring that you had a strict upbringing, by making sure that you never knew how much that one incident wrecked her whole life? We were so scared of the sins of the mother being visited on you that we overcompensated. I know now that the circumstances of your birth weren't that important. You were ours. Loving you should have been our main concern, and we failed miserably.

God gave us you, Darcy. You are our child and we will never stop loving you, no matter what has happened or will happen. Nothing can change that, my dear. Not anything.

Dad and I are so proud of you. We never told you that, I know, but it's true all the same. We felt that whatever good you did was because we'd raised you right. Now I see that your success in school was due to you and you alone, Darcy. So many times these past five years I've heard my nagging, nasty words echoing through my head, and wondered why I said them. My only excuse is that I wanted to love you and I didn't know how to tell you that. I do now. I love you, Darcy.

I tried to talk you into the adoption because I felt your baby would have a better home with a couple than with you. I was so scared. But I was wrong, Darcy. You will make an excellent mother because with you the person inside will always come first. It's strange to think of ourselves as grandparents and yet everyday we thank God for this small life He has entrusted you with. We're confident that the Lord has a special plan for your life, one we know nothing about but that is all the more wonderful because it's from Him. And He will lead you through paths I couldn't begin to understand five years ago. I think I understand them better now.

Don't feel sad when you look around, Darcy. Rejoice and be glad. If you are reading this, we're in heaven, and though I desperately wanted to hold you just one more time, to tell you that you are my very special daughter, I'm glad you're not here. I couldn't bear for you to think of me like this. Ah, my old vanity again. When will I learn that it's what is on the inside that counts?

Darcy smiled through her tears, remembering how her mother hated to have anyone see her without her nails filed, hair neatly combed, her clothing covered by a spotless white apron.

When God gave you to us, we were so happy and proud. Today I feel like that, too, because I know that the Father is watching out for my little girl. And He will be there, beside you, for the rest of your journey in this life, in spite of our mistakes.

I love you, my dear daughter. More than life itself.

Your very proud mother.

"Mommy? Why are you crying, Mommy?" Jamie patted her arm carefully, his round little face peering up in concern. "Are you sad, Mommy?" The bruising around his eye had turned to a faint yellow now, but he was walking and talking—and that's all that Darcy cared about. That and the fact that she finally understood.

"Sad—and happy, sweetheart. But I'm fine." She kissed his forehead, hugging him to her breast.

"You're squishing the paper, Mommy!" Jamie tugged out of her arms and held out a single sheet of paper. "You dropped it on the floor."

"Thank you, darling."

"Welcome." He grinned and skipped out the door to watch the end of his program.

Darcy stared down at the solid black writing, added on at the end of her mother's words. She'd never known her father to sit down and write a letter. The fact that he had apparently taken enough time to do so told her that he wanted to be sure she understood him.

Luke Lassiter is a good man, Darcy. I trust him to manage the ranch. In return for his faithful service to your mother and me when I couldn't pay him, and for all the wonderful care he and Clarice have given to us, I've deeded half the place over to him. I had hoped that one day you two might meet and that Luke would be my son-in-law. He needs someone to take care of him and you would do that very well. But I know that it's up to God and He is able to take care of you far better than we ever could. Your mother and I pray for you every night, knowing that God is watching over you and our grandchild.

> We love you, Darcy.
> Dad.

They loved her! The tears flowed steadily down her cheeks as she tried to absorb everything. They hadn't cared about what she'd done, or the fact that she had run away.

Thank you, Lord, she whispered, carefully folding the precious words and secreting them inside her purse. *Thank you so much.*

She fingered the sparkling diamond that Luke had given her. She'd tucked it into her purse for safekeeping, but now she pulled it out and set it on the desk. *Thank you for giving me this bit of solace before I leave here.*

She was so tempted to stay, to fulfil her parents' wishes.

But she needed some time to think.

Darcy tugged on her coat and took a walk down the lane. She needed to move on. But how?

"Darcy?" Jalise stared at her from inside her car. "Didn't you hear me honk?" She stared at her friend's tearstained face. "What's wrong?"

"Hi, Jalise. Nothing. *Everything.* I'm leaving Raven's Rest. Again."

"But you can't!" Jalise's eyes darkened. "Your

whole life is here. Clarice, the ranch, the school kids. Luke. He loves you, Darcy.''

Jalise motioned Darcy into the car, where it was warm, and Darcy got in before answering.

"I love him, too. But I can't stay here, Jay. Not now."

"But why? Surely you realize that God has been leading you back? He's provided you with a home, people who love you, and work that you're very good at. Why would you want to leave?"

"I have to. I'm not worthy of Luke's love." It hurt to say it, but it was the truth. "Besides, I promised."

"Promised who?" Jay frowned. "I don't understand."

"I know. I guess that's been the problem all along. How to understand Darcy!" She laughed harshly, the pain welling up inside.

"Honey, Luke doesn't care about what you've done in the past. Nobody does. All he wants is a future with you and Jamie. That's all he's wanted for months."

"He has?"

"Listen, Dar, once I thought Luke would make a good husband for me. Lord knows, I'm lonely and I don't want to spend the rest of my life alone. Running the restaurant has just been something to fill in the hours." She cleared her throat. "But Luke told me long ago that he wasn't interested. And when I see him with you, I know his love for you was meant to be. You can't run away from that kind of love any more than you could run away from your parents' love! It's right there, just waiting for you to accept it."

"I thought I could. But now I realize it was just wishful thinking." She tried to laugh and ended up sobbing. "Besides, I made a deal with God. I promised to give up everything I thought I'd found if God would just heal Jamie. He kept His part, and now it's time for me to do the same."

"Oh, Dar!" Jalise laughed in relief as the tears welled up in her eyes. "You can't make bargains with God. Nobody knows that better than me. Believe me, I tried with Billy." She hugged her friend close. "God had a plan then and He has one now. He loves you, sweetie. He's laid it all out so perfectly. You've returned home, you've won over the naysayers. You've found a place where you can serve in the community. And you found Luke."

Darcy tried to concentrate on the words, seeing the big picture form, but knowing the one fatal flaw.

"And most of all, you found love, and Jamie found a daddy. Do you think He planned all that for you to have you just walk away? God loves you, Darcy. You're His daughter, His child! He wants everything good for you. And He's given it to you. But you have to take it and do something with it."

The words hit a chord inside that had died sometime in the distant past. She was loved, in so many ways. It was what she'd always longed for, dreamed of, and it had been right here all along. Could she just throw it all away again?

"But you don't understand. I've spoiled things, made so many mistakes. I have an illegitimate child."

"You have a wonderful son, Dar. A little boy that God gave you when you needed someone to love. And you've asked for God's forgiveness, haven't you?'' She waited till Darcy nodded. ''Well, when God forgives, the Bible says He remembers *no more*. You're dwelling on something that God has already forgiven and forgotten, girl. He doesn't want you to do some kind of penance for the rest of your life just because Jamie is alive and well!''

''But can Luke forgive and forget?'' The dreaded fear grew inside her brain. ''I don't think so. He'll be reminded of my ugly past every time he looks at Jamie.''

''Oh, Darcy,'' Jalise murmured. ''Luke doesn't care about the past. He's too busy thinking about the future.''

''He might care. If he knew the truth.'' Darcy could hardly bear to think about the awful things she'd kept locked away inside. Just like her parents had hidden their secrets.

''I don't think his love is that shallow. But if *you* do, test him. Tell him the truth and see if it matters to him or not. What have you got to lose?''

Darcy thought about it for a moment. ''All right, I'll tell him. It won't be easy. I've never told anyone else.''

''But won't it be worth it to have him in your life for good?''

''Yes. Thank you, Jay.'' She threw her arms around Jalise and hugged her tightly. ''You always were the best friend in the world.''

''It took you long enough to notice,'' Jalise laughed, hugging her back. ''Now don't you have something to do?''

''Yes, I guess I do.'' Darcy got out of the car, closed the door and waved goodbye. Then she headed back toward the house, her mind busy. She wasn't going to hide the past anymore. If anyone knew better, it was her. Too much pain and sorrow had come from keeping secrets.

She hardly dared imagine that Jalise was right. Would Luke forgive her? Did God really mean for her to have it *all?*

"Mommy?" Jamie's little face peered up at her curiously, from the open front door.

"What, sweetie?"

"Are we going looking for a new home?" The blue eyes were wide and innocent, and Darcy gave thanks again to the Father who had watched over them so carefully.

"You know something, Love Bug? I think we've already found our home." Darcy glanced around, searching for some glimpse of Luke. *Please God, let me finally be home.*

"Clarice, could you keep Jamie busy for a while? I have something I need to talk to Luke about."

The older woman's face shone with an inner light as she wrapped her arms around the two of them, squeezing for all she was worth. When she let them go at last, her eyes sparkled with unshed tears of joy.

"He's out in the workshop, love."

Darcy hurried to Luke's private workshop. He was inside, bent over something on the worktable. She slipped through the door soundlessly and waited, content to watch his big, capable hands tenderly sand the hard wood.

"Luke."

He whirled around, his face anguished-looking.

"Darcy? I thought you were packing. Did you forget something?"

She heard the pain in his words even though he strove to hide it. Her heart ached for the trouble she'd caused him and she vowed to make up for it. For the rest of her life.

"Yes, I did. I forgot a lot of things." She stood where she was, imprinting the strong features on her mind forever. "I forgot to trust God. I forgot to trust you. I forgot that the truth kept hidden can only hurt. And, worst of all, I forgot about love. I was hoping you could listen to something I need to say."

He nodded, his eyes brimming with curiosity.

"I know you don't understand why I thought I had to leave, so I'd like to explain something. It happened a long time ago."

"It doesn't matter, Darcy. I don't care about the past. I've got my hope in the future. But if it will make you feel better, go ahead. I'll listen."

"Thank you." She drew a huge breath, plopped down on a stump and began. "You already know that I was the town brat. It seemed to me as if everyone hated me, and I could understand that. I hated myself. But Josiah Pringle was the one boy who saw through my bad-girl image to the insecure child underneath. He took time to talk to me, encourage me, hold me when I cried. I thought he loved me.

"We spent a lot of time together. Secret time when my parents thought I was locked up in my room. They had grounded me because of some gossip by a woman in the church. They didn't care that I was innocent, or maybe they knew better. Anyway, one afternoon I snuck out and met Josiah at this secret place we had in the woods.'' Darcy forced herself to meet his gaze.

"I was so angry, and so *hurt*. How could they believe that I was a tramp? My own parents? Josiah comforted me as he always had, only this time he got carried away. I thought, 'Well, why not? Maybe it will make him love me more.''' She laughed bitterly.

"It didn't. He ran off and left me there, and I suddenly realized that I had become everything they'd called me.'' She felt the tears rolling down her cheeks, but ignored them, needing to get it all said. "Several weeks later I figured out that I was pregnant. I sent Josiah a note, which his mother read. She brought him along to our meeting and proceeded to tell me that Josiah wasn't going to be tied to the town 'harlot.' Besides, she said, how could they be sure the baby was his?''

"What did he say?'' Luke's voice was full of anger.

"Nothing. He stood there staring at the floor and let her tear me to shreds. She threatened to tell my parents the whole story unless I had an abortion.''

"What!''

"I couldn't do it. I knew I'd done wrong. And I knew I had to pay for it. But I couldn't take my baby's life!'' She remembered the agony of decision. "Josiah promised we'd get married after graduation. We could have another baby. He'd be free then—of legal age. So I agreed. Or pretended to. His mother never said a word to me. He probably told her that I'd had the abortion.''

"But you didn't.'' It wasn't a question.

"No, I couldn't. I kept thinking that the baby

hadn't done anything wrong. I had. I should pay, not the baby. When we graduated, I made sure I was top of the class. I poured myself into getting those grades, as if that would help. But I was still pregnant, and I knew it wouldn't be long before I showed. I talked to Josiah just once, the last time I saw him. He said he had met someone else. A 'good Christian' girl. They were serious. So I went to my parents and I told them I was pregnant.''

Luke frowned. ''They never knew whose baby it was?''

''No.'' She shook her head.

He moved toward her, his hand gentle on her shoulder. ''But Darcy, none of it matters, don't you see? It's the past. And thanks to your grit, you have Jamie. Was that *his* middle name?''

''James was his father's middle name. I had some dream of a tradition, you see.'' She smiled grimly, mocking her own foolishness, as her fingers wrapped tightly around his. ''I was a fool.''

''So who isn't?'' He kissed the top of her head, his arms around her. ''But why did you suddenly decide to leave? Was it something I said?''

''No!'' She snuggled her head into his shoulder. ''It was something I felt. Guilt. A great big load of it. I thought Jamie's getting hurt was God's way of getting even with me for my sin—sort of a payback. I reasoned that if I agreed to give up everything I loved, God would forgive me enough to let Jamie live.''

Luke gently pressed her away, his eyes serious. ''Sweetheart, God doesn't treat His children like that.

He's forgiven you for the past. I think it's time you forgave yourself.''

Darcy smiled up at him. ''I was kind of hoping you'd remind me.'' She waited expectantly, praying that Jalise hadn't been wrong.

''Are you sure this time? Really sure, Darcy?'' His arms moved up around her, gently cuddling her closer.

''I'd like to take you up on your offer of marriage, Luke. If you still want me, that is.''

''For how long?'' he whispered, drawing a shaky breath.

''I thought maybe—'' she paused ''—for the rest of our lives. I've finally come home, Luke. I'm not really Martha and Lester's daughter. I'm just me, God's child and Jamie's mom. And maybe, just maybe, your wife.''

His melting brown eyes slid over her, absorbing every detail, before his arms tightened. ''Thank God!'' And then he kissed her with a thoroughness that left her in no doubt of his feelings on the matter.

And Darcy, with her heart singing heavenly music, kissed him back.

Epilogue

"Darcy, you've got to stand still if you want me to get this hat on straight. The veiling is lopsided," Jalise murmured in frustration.

"I don't even care if I *have* a veil," Darcy replied. "I don't know why I let Luke talk me into all this fuss anyway. We could have been married without all the hoopla. I only ever agreed to marry the man—not to let the town watch!"

"That's about to happen in less than five minutes, so you'd better make the best of it." Clarice straightened the ivory lace that trailed behind. "Besides, my nephew wanted you to have this special day to look back on for years and years. And I think he was right."

"So do I." Jalise nodded, satisfied with her work.

"You look lovely, dear. I'm sure your mother is looking down from heaven, smiling right now. She always meant for you to wear her dress." Clarice fingered the old silk gently. "She'd be so proud of you today."

"I know. I wish Dad was here to walk me down the aisle." Darcy smiled, feeling the thrill in her heart that the hurt was finally gone. "I guess he probably is, even if I can't see him."

"Everybody's here," Jalise said, glancing between the curtains. "Even Mrs. Lancaster!"

Darcy peeked, too. The music changed and Luke's brother, who was serving as the best man, entered the church, followed by Jamie and then Luke. They looked so handsome as they lined up in front in their matching black suits and bow ties.

"Come on, woman! It's time for us to meet that fiancé of yours and his bossy brother." Jalise spread the short wispy tulle over Darcy's shoulders and smoothed the full ruffled skirt. "You look beautiful, Dar. I love you." She pressed a kiss against Darcy's cheek and accepted a hug in return.

Darcy took a deep breath, relishing the words. *I love you.* It was so wonderful to hear that. She would never tire of it. Never. And she was learning to give as good as she got.

"I love you, Jay. And you, too, Clarice." She smiled mistily. "I feel like I'm overflowing with love."

Jalise grinned. "I think that big lug at the front feels the same way. Look at his grin." She made a face. "It's too bad his best man couldn't smile a little more. Cade Lassiter is nothing like his brother!"

"Now Jay, no fighting. It's not nice. Besides, I don't want to play peacemaker between you two."

"You won't have time. That's the prelude Gertie's

using to signal you. Get moving. Go on out there and tie up that groom nice and tight before someone else does.'' Clarice pushed them out the door, grasped the usher's arm, and marched beside him to her seat near the front.

As the chords of the ''Wedding March'' resounded through the small building, Jalise gave Darcy's hand one last squeeze, picked up her bouquet of daffodils and started down the aisle. Little Ginny Jones followed her, walking carefully with her new braces. When she reached the front, Darcy tightened her fingers around her own bouquet of spring iris, lilies and daffodils, and stepped out slowly, her eyes firmly fixed on the tall, lean man with the glowing brown eyes that twinkled a secret message.

''Hi, beautiful.'' His fingers gathered hers in a squeeze of reassurance. ''You look wonderful, Darcy.''

''So do you.'' More than wonderful, she wanted to say. Like a dream come true. And her heart sang praises to God.

The old-fashioned vows were savored and repeated all through the congregation as the bride and groom promised their love to each other. René Jones's poignant solo left not a dry eye in the church. And the townsfolk of Raven's Rest spent many an hour after the reception discussing how wonderful it was that Darcy Simms had come home at last.

* * * * *

Dear Reader,

Isn't it awful to be left hanging, wondering if you matter to anyone at all? To wait, day after day, for some sign of relief from those problems that just won't quit? We moan and groan, blame other people and push ourselves to find a way out when all the time God is there, waiting for us, revealing His perfect will. I hope you've enjoyed Darcy's story and learned with her that God hasn't turned His back on you. Please watch for a return of Darcy with her friend Jalise Peters and Luke's rebel brother Cade.

Until we meet again, I wish you the steadfast assurance and calm certainty that no matter what your life brings, you are God's dear child and He will heal your heart's deepest ache.

Lois
Richer